Barbara Delinsky

CHANCES ARE

Harlequin Books

TORONTO • NEW YORK • LONDON
AMSTERDAM • PARIS • SYDNEY • HAMBURG
STOCKHOLM • ATHENS • TOKYO • MILAN
MADRID • WARSAW • BUDAPEST • AUCKLAND

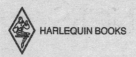 HARLEQUIN BOOKS

CHANCES ARE
© 1985 by Barbara Delinsky

ISBN 0-373-83250-8

First Harlequin Books printing October 1985

Reprinted September 1992

Printed in U.S.A.

1

HE WASN'T AT ALL what she'd expected of a prominent businessman. For one thing he was holding court in a converted mill, rather than a sleek skyscraper. For another, he wore a crew-neck sweater, soft jeans and sneakers, rather than the traditional three-piece suit. For a third, his hair was longer than the current Park Avenue style, generously brushing his forehead and the collar of his plaid shirt, which edged above his sweater. It was his voice, though, not deep and authoritative but quiet and gentle, that stunned her most—stunned her and mesmerized her as it flowed over the group of foreign businessmen who had come to hear the guru speak.

Lingering near the entrance of the barnlike room where the nation's latest craze—a game called Chimera—was produced, Elizabeth Jerome focused in on the discussion.

"Throughout history people have been drawn to games," Donovan Grant was saying. "They're a form of relaxation, a challenge on a plane less threatening than, say, a job or even a marriage. Board games such as backgammon and chess have been around for centuries. Even more modern ones like Scrabble and Monopoly have become mainstays in modern homes."

One of the visitors spoke up in heavily accented English. "But the market is glutted with games today. What makes yours different?"

"Mine requires nothing more than a pair of dice, a few simple guidelines, and the imagination of the players. It involves fantasy yet appeals to the intellect, where so many recent ones have failed. It challenges the independent mind, the mind that thrives on stimulation and adventure rather than sheer luck. Chimera lets the players determine the nature and scope of the game. This gives them a sense of self-determination, a sense of control that may be lacking in their everyday lives."

Another of the foreigners interrupted, seeming mildly disgruntled to have found himself in an old mill listening to a laid-back genius discuss his latest baby. "But this has little to do with big business and the American corporation today."

Donovan turned to him with a smile Liz found to be disarming. "That's where you're wrong. The theory behind the success of Chimera applies to big business, as well."

"We have all read your book, Mr. Grant," a third guest injected. "We have come to hear your theories of economic strategy."

"Precisely," Donovan said smoothly, shifting more comfortably against the long table on which several cartons of Chimera kits lay. "There's the old economy, the traditional one, involving mass production aimed at mass consumption. And there's the new economy, in which the amount of energy used is honed down, markets are streamlined, jobs are accomplished much more efficiently. Chimera emulates the new economy,

forcing players to accomplish a goal by the most efficient means. In a sense it's a learning experience. A
player is forced to be more ingenious than his oppo-
nents in order to win. That, very simply, is the secret
to success in business today."

The men listened, growing progressively enrapt as
he continued to speak softly, elaborating on his economic theory. Several times he gave specific examples,
timely examples that dated even his own book. Liz was
as fascinated as the others by the time the session ended
and the businessmen moved forward to shake the hand
of the man responsible for shaping any number of successful business ventures in the past decade. She stayed
where she was, though, until the last of the group had
filed past and the wizard himself approached.

"You must be Elizabeth Jerome," he said in that same
fluid tone he'd used to charm his visitors.

Once again she marveled at his manner, so unlike
that of corporate heads she'd dealt with in the past. She
wondered if it was all an act, but when he offered his
hand and a smile as relaxed as he seemed, she aban-
doned that idea and swallowed hard.

"That's right," she managed, returning his warm
handshake with one that was as firm, if more prac-
ticed. She tossed her head toward the door. "Very im-
pressive. You took adversity and turned it around. I'm
glad to have witnessed it."

His smile grew crooked. "I really didn't plan it that
way. I wasn't expecting you until noon."

"I managed to catch an earlier flight to Albany," she
explained, gently extricating her hand from his. He was
staring at her, in his first show of something other than

nonchalance, and she wasn't sure why. Uncomfortable, she averted her gaze to make a cursory study of the massive room. "Your driver was early, too. Thank you for sending him. Why did you pick Troy for this plant, when the rest of your interests are in Manhattan?"

"Manhattan grates after a while. I need the breather. I guess I'm a small-town boy at heart."

She looked back in time to see him grin, and she felt suddenly and strangely vulnerable. He had dimples in his cheeks; their flash seemed to ricochet through her insides. "A small-town boy?" she asked, masking unsureness with skepticism. "But business is your forte. You've made a mark on many large corporations besides your own."

"I don't know about that," he murmured, then took her elbow and lowered his voice to a playful drawl. "Come to my office, my dear. Let me show you my etchings."

She knew he was kidding but she was more ill at ease than ever. He must have felt the tension in her body, for he dropped his hand and stepped before her to lead the way.

His office was little more than a miniature version of the room they'd just left. Its walls were of aged bare brick, bruised at spots. A single file cabinet stood against one, a desk—actually an ancient pine door on sawhorses—against another. The only concession to modernity was a computer, which occupied its own suitably sturdy stand against the third.

Gesturing to one chair, Donovan slid into the only other in the room, a desk model that stood on wheels and swiveled across the oak planks of the floor as he moved closer to her. He leaned forward, propping his forearms on his outspread knees.

"Have you been with Karen long?" he asked.

Liz sat with her legs crossed and her hands anchored neatly in her lap. She prayed that she looked professional. The pose, complemented by the gray suit she wore, had always worked before. But something about the way Donovan Grant's eyes penetrated hers made her feel awkward, as though her legs were too tightly crossed and her hands positively stiff in repose. "Six years," she answered quietly. "I came to her right from graduate school."

"You have a degree in public relations?"

"Yes." She took a quick breath, fearing he had doubts of her ability. "I assure you I'm well qualified to handle your problem. I've handled other sticky ones—"

"I know," he interrupted succinctly, then smiled and leaned back in his chair. "Karen gave me a rundown on the clients you've represented when she recommended you." He paused, staring again. "Relax. I won't bite, y'know."

She looked away, then back. "I know. It's just that . . . well, you're very . . . different."

He cocked his head. "In what way?"

"Your clothes. Your manner. I'd expected much more formality."

"Karen didn't tell you about me?" he asked with such tongue-in-cheek caution that Liz couldn't help but be curious. Only later did it occur to her that he might have intended just that.

"She told me about the DIG Group and about the problem you've got. I'd already read about it in the papers."

"She didn't tell you that we knew each other?"

"She mentioned that you were old friends, but she didn't go into detail." When his eyes began to twinkle, Liz prodded. "Where *did* you meet?"

"In college. In the sixties. We were both revolutionaries of sorts."

"Karen . . . a revolutionary?" Liz conjured an image of her boss and friend, but it was one of sophistication and conventionality. "I don't believe it."

The grin he bestowed upon her was boyish, almost naughty. "She was right there beside me during more than one peace demonstration, waving her sign, holding her ground as staunchly as the rest of us." He shook his head. "She was a vision. Long black hair hanging straight down her back, torn jeans, bare feet, loose peasant shirt with no bra underneath..." He gave a low growl that spoke of his remembered attraction as no words could better do.

Before she knew what she was saying, Liz heard herself ask, "Were you two together? Oh, Lord, I'm sorry. That's none of my business."

"It's okay," he countered easily. "I invited it. We were together for a while, but I haven't seen her in years." His voice took on that same boyish quality that his grin had conveyed moments before. It was a perfectly natural intonation, enthusiastic and innocent. "What does she look like now?"

It was Liz's turn to smile. "Her hair is still black, but it's short and sleek. She wears silk dresses, imported leather heels and I believe she's taken to wearing a . . . bra. But, if you haven't seen her in so long, what possessed you to call her yesterday?"

"It's part of my philosophy, much as I was trying to tell that group a little while ago. To be successful today you've got to be smart, which means identifying weaknesses and then moving to strengthen them in the most efficient way possible. Karen Reynolds's firm is the best. I may not have been in personal touch with Karen over the years, but I'm well aware of her reputation. I like it better when you smile."

"Excuse me?"

"You smiled a minute ago. It was pretty. But now you're frowning. Did I say something wrong?"

Liz ignored his compliment without a second thought. "I'm wondering if you're disappointed that Karen sent me."

"Why on earth would I be disappointed?" he asked with genuine puzzlement.

"I'm not Karen."

Donovan could see that she wasn't Karen, yet there was definitely something familiar about her. He decided that it had to be her hair, which was a warm shade of brown, worn parted in the center and flowing down her back. There was a simplicity about it, an unadorned attractiveness reminiscent of days gone by, so unusual to the modern career woman. Her eyes captivated him even more. They were hazel and, as true windows of the soul, bore an intelligence that appealed to him, a hint of defiance that intrigued him.

"You've been trained by her and she thought you'd do the best job for me. I never expected that she'd personally handle this. In fact, if she'd suggested it, I'd have been skeptical."

"Why?"

"Because I want your full attention. I'll *need* it if this job's going to be done right. Karen is an administrator. She's got to keep tabs on many things at once if she's going to keep her organization operating smoothly. You don't have those administrative duties to dilute the time you give to me."

Something in his words made Liz uneasy. Or maybe it wasn't his words as much as his eyes. They were penetrating again, demanding in a way that neither his voice nor his casual pose suggested. If she'd been another woman, she might have been tempted to add deeper meaning to his words. But she wasn't another woman. She was Elizabeth Jerome. Plain, professional Elizabeth Jerome.

At the personal reminder, she sat straighter. "Let's talk about what you need done."

"Right." But he was out of his chair and grabbing her hand to draw her with him toward the door. "Over lunch. I'm starved."

She had no choice but to follow him, half trotting to keep up with his strides. When she was tucked safely in the passenger seat of his sporty Audi, he slid behind the wheel.

"Nice car...for an ex-revolutionary," she commented with a grin. She couldn't picture him in the role of the corporate giant, and she was content, under the guise of professional research, to explore the man himself. Knowing what made him tick would be invaluable if she was to be his champion in the weeks to come.

"Revolutionaries grow up," he said good-naturedly as he started the car and headed from the parking lot. "We also develop tastes for the good life. Oh, our personalities don't change; we still like to be different. But we learn to temper our urges, to channel them appropriately."

"Then you've sworn off demonstrations?"

"Not completely. If I believed very strongly in a cause and felt that a public demonstration was the most effective statement, I'd be out there marching. But I have alternatives now. I have more influence, power, if you will, to affect things. It's a matter of working from the inside to change what I believe is wrong."

"Is that what your consulting is about?"

He shot her a glance. "You know about that? You've done your homework."

"Only in the broadest sense, with the resources that were at my disposal at the last minute. I know, obviously, that you're involved with health foods, and that you've got a thriving courier service and a commuter airline. But from what I've read, it's the consulting you're really known for. A cult following?"

His mouth slanted on the mild side of a grimace. "I wouldn't call it that exactly. It's just that people are always looking to grab on to something—or someone—who can give them hope. I get calls all the time from would-be entrepreneurs wondering if one scheme or another of theirs is worth pursuing. More often than not I tell them to forget it, but even that impresses them."

"You're being too modest," Liz chided. "Much of the consulting you do is on a larger scale. You've been called in by some of the largest corporations in the country to make suggestions on how they can better manage their interests."

"Their interests are monstrosities, which is the major source of the problem. Unchecked growth gets quickly out of hand. The right doesn't know what the left is doing. It doesn't take genius to see that or to tell them to streamline. Where are you from, Elizabeth Jerome?"

The abrupt shift in conversation, accompanied as it was by no shift in tone, took her off guard for a minute. She blinked once, then steadied herself. "Baltimore, originally. Tell me about your interest in health foods."

He cast her a quick glance, but acquiesced. His hands were relaxed on the wheel; the car seemed little more than a smoothly operating extension of the man himself. "Health foods and I go way back. In my early, uh, nonconformist days, I was often in the midst of discussions about chemical additives in foods. When I finally realized I was going to have to do something to earn a living, it seemed only natural that I should turn to the manufacture and marketing of organically grown products. Actually, luck had more than a little to do with my success. Luck, and timing, and patience. I got into the field just early enough to find my sources and set up an efficient operation before the American public tuned in to health foods. I was there and ready when the market mushroomed."

"Was it luck or foresight?"

He shrugged. "I wish I could say it was foresight, but at the time I wasn't exactly into making money. I was still pretty much of a hippie."

"But you knew enough to do things right."

"I suppose that was instinct, though I only recognized it later. I started with a single small outlet in Los Angeles and would have been satisfied at the time if it had simply given me enough to live on. When it did better than that, the challenge grew. I contracted more growers and opened a second outlet, then a third and so on. It was like a game, and I was calling the shots. Before I'd realized it, I'd become a full-fledged entrepreneur."

"And today? How large is the business?"

"I've got processing plants in six states, better than ninety thousand acres of land being planted, nearly a thousand employees and a source network that extends to a dozen foreign countries. It's pretty large, I guess."

"Large enough to inspire sabotage," Liz commented thoughtfully. Donovan held up a hand in a gesture that might have been harsh had it not been delivered simultaneously with a smile. "Not yet. I can't discuss that on an empty stomach. When did you leave Baltimore, Elizabeth?"

She wanted to say that everyone called her Liz, but she didn't. There was something about the way her full name flowed from his tongue that made it sound pretty to her as it never had. There was also something warm and comforting about him that quelled any objection she might have had to this detour from business. "When I went off to college."

"Where did you go?"

"Emery."

"In Atlanta? That's a great place!"

"I got a good education there."

"And the graduate degree?"

"Boston University."

"Had you always wanted to work in Manhattan?"

"Only once I realized that the best jobs were there." She glanced out the window of the car to find that they'd long since left the urban confines of Troy and were traveling along a road bordered by open fields and trees. "Where are we going?"

"My place. I make the best cheeseburgers around."

Liz tensed, only realizing by contrast how slyly Donovan Grant had put her at ease. "I, uh, we could have grabbed something in town." She didn't look at him. She didn't dare. But she heard the smile in his words and knew he was laughing at her.

"I felt this would be better. We need privacy for what we have to discuss."

"We could have stayed in your office."

"Nah. Too impersonal."

"This is an impersonal issue."

"I certainly hope not!"

When Liz's gaze flew to his in alarm, she met a pair of dancing brown eyes. But the dancing abruptly ceased when Donovan sensed her fright.

"It's okay," he soothed, though he was clearly puzzled. "I was only talking about work. It is a personal issue—for me at least." He paused, darting intermittent glances at Liz as she gnawed on her lower lip. "You're edgy. Do men come on to you often?"

"No!" She'd never had to worry about come-ons...or double entendres...or embarrassment, which was what she felt most noticeably now. A man like Donovan Grant—successful, charming and good-looking to boot—wouldn't be interested in her. Why she'd even jumped to the conclusion she had she couldn't fathom. "I just like to stick to business."

"You don't ever mix work with fun?"

"No." She sat straight-faced, staring out the windshield.

"Not even a little?" His voice was higher, teasing.

Liz realized she was making too much out of nothing, and she forced herself to relax. "No," she said more quietly. It was just as well he knew at the start where she stood. She didn't think she could bear being humiliated by someone as bright, as confident, as handsome as the man at the wheel.

"That's a shame," he said very softly, almost to himself, then raised his voice. "What *do* you do for fun?"

She shrugged the edge off her unease. "The same things other people do."

"Like...?"

"Read. Eat out. Go to the theater."

"Alone?"

"Sometimes. Sometimes not. Tell me more about the DIG Group. Anything else beside the courier service, the airline and health foods?"

"Chimera. Have you ever played?"

"No. I went to buy it once but the store was sold out." She looked over at him. "There's been a shortage. Was that intentional?"

"Not really, though it did serve to whet the public's appetite. We really hadn't anticipated the demand, or rather, we'd planned conservatively at the start. Production's been stepped up, though, so the problem should be solved. I'll give you a kit and some booklets with potential scenarios before you leave."

"That's not necessary. I can buy—"

"I'd like to *give* them to you. Consider it an advance on payment for your services."

Again Liz felt a tremor of discomfort. Something about the way he'd spoken of services conjured other images. She told herself that she was being neurotic and wondered why she couldn't simply take this man at face value. Perhaps it was because his tone of voice was somehow intimate, or because his gaze penetrated her each time it left the road. Then again, perhaps it was her own very foolish imagination.

"Where are we now?" she asked, needing to steer the talk along less threatening lines.

Again Donovan yielded, though not before he'd thrown her a knowing glance. "We're heading northwest. If we were to continue in this direction we'd hit the Adirondacks. Ever explore them?"

"No. I hear they're beautiful."

"The park itself is the largest of its kind in the country. Six million acres in northern New York. It's also considered to be one of the most beautiful. The northern areas are less traveled and almost completely unspoiled. As inhospitable as they can be in bad weather, they're breathtaking when tackled properly."

Liz swiveled in her seat to study him more easily. "You've tackled them?"

"Only parts. I'll cover them all if I live long enough. There's something about hiking through dense woods, around and over mountains. I mean, we may not be talking the Rockies, but the wilderness here is every bit as inspiring. When you're out there alone surrounded by nothing but the sights and sounds of nature . . ." His voice trailed off and he breathed a soft growl not unlike the one he'd made when recalling Karen Reynolds's braless past.

Liz had to smile. "So it's not just women who turn you on?"

The corner of his lips twitched. "Not by a long shot. Nature turns me on. So does business. In different ways than a good woman would, of course."

"Of course."

"Where was I?"

"A geography lesson."

"Ah, a geography lesson. The male physique—"

"Of the Adirondacks."

"Mmm. Actually, the other's just as interesting."

"It's irrelevant."

"Now just a minute. I wouldn't say that my body's irrelevant." He dropped a fast glance to the subject in question. "The male geography can be—"

"The Adirondacks?" Liz interrupted in gently pointed reminder. But she'd begun to relax again and took no offense in the sexual banter. "If you refuse to discuss business, the least you can do is to educate me a little."

"That's what I was trying to do," he countered innocently.

"The Adirondacks . . . ?"

He set his lips in mock show of discipline. "Right." He took a breath. "The Adirondacks cover six million acres—"

"You've told me that."

"I have? Oh. Okay, where did I leave off when I was so rudely interrupted?"

"You weren't rudely interrupted."

"I was, too. *You* were the one who raised the subject of turn-ons."

"Only when you started to pant at mention of the wilderness."

"The wilderness. Okay, let's take it from there. Did you know that the human body is a wilderness—self-generating, sustained directly or indirectly by the sun, filled with nooks and crannies waiting to be explored?"

Liz dropped her head to her hands and shook it slowly. For a split second Donovan was mesmerized by the shimmer of her hair, so clean and soft and natural, striking that familiar chord in him. Then he heeded her gesture. He spoke quickly, though, as if he desperately wanted to be done with this particular geography lesson.

"The southern areas of the Adirondacks were heavily logged in the 1800s. Fortunately much of the forest has grown back, though old logging roads still wind through it. Small pockets of privately owned land intermingle with what the government now owns, but even the private landowners are protective."

"Do you live in one of those pockets?"

"Couldn't get one. Private landowners are not only protective but possessive. Here, this is my road." He'd slowed the car and was turning off onto a narrow strip of rutted pavement. Had Liz been alone she might have completely missed the road, hidden as it was by thickly canopied growth. Pines and hemlocks were interspersed with deciduous trees whose leaves had just begun their autumnal change.

"This is country!" Liz remarked appreciatively. "It's hard to believe we're less than an hour's flying time from Manhattan."

"That's what's so fantastic about living here."

"Do you commute daily?"

"To and from the city? No. I have a place there, but this is my haven."

"Some haven," she crooned in envy. They were cruising slowly down the road, which showed no sign of ending. "Where is the house?"

"Another three-quarters of a mile."

"My Lord, how do you manage when it snows?"

"I'm plowed out. And this car's got four-wheel drive. Not that there haven't been a couple of hairy times . . ."

"I can imagine. You're really isolated out here, aren't you?"

"Yup. And I live alone." He looked at her. "No wife. No girlfriend. No housekeeper."

"Are you trying to scare me?"

"Nope. Just want you to know I'm available."

"But I'm not."

"You're not married."

She flexed the bare fingers of her left hand and lowered her eyes to study them. "No. But we have a business relationship. It can't be anything more."

"Why not?"

The innocent way he'd asked brought her gaze back up, but he was concentrating on negotiating the increasingly winding, occasionally hilly road. She felt an inkling of annoyance that he should tease her so.

"Because."

"Because why?"

Because I'm plain and you're gorgeous. Because I'm inexperienced and you've been around. Because I'm spinster material and you'll be snatched up before long. "Just . . . because."

"Not good enough."

"Where *is* this place of yours, anyway?"

"Right . . . there."

Sure enough, a house suddenly materialized from amid the forest. It was built of stone and looked like a relic of bygone days, except it was dated by huge expanses of windows and a skylight or two.

Enchanted, Liz promptly forgot all annoyance. "It's charming," she breathed.

"Thank you. I like it." Bringing the car to a full stop, he swung from behind the wheel and trotted around to help her out. The hand that took her elbow slid down to firmly grasp her hand. She didn't resist as he buoyantly led her up the walk.

The inside of the house was delightful, if slightly disorderly. Even Donovan seemed taken aback by the newspapers and magazines that graced the upholstered sofa and the sweat suit that was flung over the arm of one chair.

"Uh, sorry about this." He gathered the papers together in one large sweep and anchored them under his arm. "I hadn't anticipated having guests."

Liz wanted to ask him what he *had* anticipated. He'd known she was coming. If he'd originally planned on a lunch meeting in Troy, why was she here? But he had scooped the sweat suit from the chair and was off before she could say a thing.

"Make yourself comfortable," he called over his shoulder. "I'll go put the meat in the microwave to defrost. It'll only take a minute."

Wary of making herself too comfortable, Liz simply stood where she was, hands clenched around the top of her oversized purse as she looked around the room. It was large, decorated sparsely but with warm things—the upholstered furniture was beige-and-navy plaid and cushiony, the pictures on the walls were of local origin and decidedly homey, the high bookshelves were crammed with volumes arranged in haphazard fashion. A low glass table stood atop a rag rug that lay atop the highly polished wood floor. A large fireplace, its grate covered with ashes, broke up one wall. Beside it was a basket of logs.

In an open loft high above was another sofa, a television and a stereo. Books and magazines littered this area, as well, but they merely enhanced the lived-in look that gave the house such charm.

The sounds of activity in the kitchen brought Liz's attention back to the ground floor. She was tempted to follow the noise, then thought better of it and slowly edged toward one of the armchairs and settled cautiously into it. She folded her hands in her lap. She looked around. Her eye fell on the bookshelf again and she left her chair to peruse the books it held. Some of the volumes related to business, but the bulk covered other diverse topics. There were books on travel, books on art, books on mountain climbing, books on self-improvement. And there were novels—many of which she'd read herself—both recent and not.

"Ah," came a voice from close behind her, and she jumped. "You're studying my collection. Even better than etchings. You can learn a whole lot about a man by what he reads."

"So I was thinking," she murmured, then firmed up her voice. "Every little bit helps if I'm to represent you well."

Donovan's arm brushed her shoulder when he reached behind her to finger the binding of one particular book. "You're not going to announce to the world that I read escapist literature, are you?"

She stepped aside and looked back at the shelf. "There's nothing wrong with it, though I really liked the book L'Amour wrote before that one better."

"You read him, too?" Donovan asked in surprise.

"Doesn't everyone?"

"But I thought men mainly liked westerns."

"Now that," she said with a grin, "is a sexist comment if I've ever heard one. And coming from a former hippie, it's shocking."

The book forgotten, he was concentrating on her face. Her eyes were gentle, almost shy despite the surface boldness of her grin. She seemed a rarity amid the ultrasophistication of New York. "I like to shock. It's part of the game."

Liz grew uneasy then. He was standing far too close, studying her far too intently. She wanted to run, to escape, to hide, but her purpose in being there held her rooted to the spot. "What game?" she asked nervously.

"Life. Love."

When the last word slid from his mobile lips, she did bolt. Quickly crossing the room, she leaned against the back of the chair in which she'd rested moments before. She didn't like games, particularly ones dealing with love. Or lust. Or physical need. Or whatever the head player chose to call it.

Donovan followed her flight, unrelenting in his scrutiny. She darted him a glance, then looked away and was about to remind him of the purpose of their meeting when he spoke softly.

"I didn't mean to frighten you. I seem to do that a lot, though, don't I?"

"I'm not frightened."

"Then threatened. Why?"

"I'm not threatened," she lied.

"Call it what you will, but the fact remains that I make you nervous. I don't understand, Elizabeth. You're an attractive woman. Surely you're used to men who tease."

You're an attractive woman. You're an attractive woman. "I don't like teasing. Look, maybe you should be working with someone else from the office. I could go back and speak to Karen—"

"I don't want to work with someone else. I want to work with you."

"But we've obviously hit an impasse—"

"You're the one who's hit an impasse. I don't see any problem. I'm not going to jump you and ravish you on the floor. And I really didn't have anything sinister in mind when I brought you here, unless you call getting to know someone better sinister. Maybe if you try to relax, to take my teasing with a grain of salt, you'll find that I'm a nice guy after all."

She met his gaze with some hesitancy. "You are a nice guy. It's just that . . . well, I guess I'm not used to teasing. It makes me uncomfortable."

He thought for a minute. "I can handle that." He took a step toward her, then stopped. "Can you cook?"

She frowned for just an instant before realizing that, in the way that appeared to be characteristic of him, Donovan was changing the subject. "Not in the gourmet sense."

"Good." He resumed walking, but back toward the kitchen. "Then I don't have to worry that you'll cringe when you see what I mix with the hamburg." He was about to gesture for her to follow when he glanced back, paused, then backtracked to gently pry her fingers from her bag and set the latter on the chair. "Come," was all he said before he left her alone.

Liz half wished he'd taken her hand, as he'd done several times that day, and led her. Then she wouldn't have had a choice. As things stood now, she had to decide whether to be a coward and remain in the living room or to trust Donovan. With a deep breath she pulled herself up straight. She was twenty-nine, independent and professional. If it was instinct that advised trust, it was that sense of professionalism that gave her the courage to move.

Donovan's back was to her when she appeared at the door of the kitchen. He was rummaging in a cabinet, extracting one bottle, then another and several spice tins. His momentary distraction gave her time to examine her surroundings, which she did with growing pleasure.

This was no backwoods stove-and-icebox kitchen, but rather a thoroughly modern, well-equipped room containing a double oven, a separately mounted microwave, abundant cabinet space and spacious countertops. The far end of the room opened into a dining area made bright by hip-to-ceiling windows. Just as in the living room, there were no drapes to shield the sunlight, which streamed freely over the lacquered table and across the ceramic-tiled floor.

"Okay?" Donovan asked. His expression held a hint of unsureness.

"It's great!" Liz responded readily. Though his question and its attendant gaze lent deeper meaning to his inquiry, she concentrated on the room. "You must have done a lot of work when you bought this place. I didn't expect anything as modern."

He ran his hand along the shiny countertop. "I figured that if it was food that earned me the down payment on this place, I'd better show respect in the kitchen."

"Since when do cheeseburgers qualify as health food?"

His lean cheeks grew flushed, but only for an instant. "I'm not the fanatic I used to be. Besides, lean meat and cheese provide protein for a balanced diet. I mean, I buy the best, stuff that's not piled with preservatives, and I won't be offering you marshmallow fluff on the side. We can have fresh fruit for dessert. In fact, I may slice some fresh carrots to go with the burgers. I love raw carrots. They're great munchies. Don't look at me that way. They *are* good."

"For rabbits."

"Don't knock 'em. Rabbits are healthy little creatures. They're sure as hell good at reproducing ... don't *look* at me that way." He gave a low growl, this time in frustration. "I'm beyond redemption. Face it. I've got a one-track mind."

"Mmm. But you can switch tracks. I've seen you do it. Maybe if we talk about the maniac who poisoned your fields—"

Donovan held up a hand. "Uh! Not yet. First, we eat."

Liz raised a brow and eyed the raw hamburg he'd just removed from the microwave. "First, you'd better cook, don't you think?"

"Cook. Right." He slid the miscellaneous whatevers he'd taken from the cabinet across the counter to the hamburg, reached into another cabinet for a mixing bowl and began to work. "Have a seat and tell me about your life."

She walked to the table, slid into a chair and held herself straight. "I already have."

"Where do you live? Co-op? Apartment? House? In the city or out of it?"

"If I lived in a suburb, I wouldn't be as green with envy over this place. No, I've got an apartment in the city."

"Do you walk to work?" His back was to her and he was dumping things into the mixing bowl with such abandon that Liz wondered if she *should* supervise.

Unfortunately that would have meant being near him, and she valued the distance.

"In good weather, yes. Otherwise I take a bus."

"What are your work hours like?"

Had he been looking at her in that intense way of his, she might have evaded the directness of his questioning. But his attention was on his work and his curiosity seemed so totally innocent that she didn't have the heart to rebuff him. "Pretty sporadic. I'm a morning person, so I try to get in early every day. Dinners with clients— or with people to be courted on behalf of clients—keep me working late. When I travel I lose track of *all* time."

His arms were working at blending the mess he'd concocted. "You like traveling?"

"I love it. Seeing different parts of the country, meeting new people—it's exciting."

"Did you travel with your family when you were growing up?"

She paused for an instant and chose her words with care. "Yes, but never with the kind of freedom I have now."

"There can't be much freedom when you're working on a case." He began to form his mixture into patties with the verve of a child making snowballs. Liz wondered at the energy he poured into it and found herself suddenly eager to taste these cheeseburgers.

"Some cases, some trips, are more demanding than others. I can usually find time to do a little sightseeing, a little shopping."

"You like to shop?"

"For other people." She smiled. "There's always someone who's got a birthday or an anniversary or some other kind of milestone coming up. If I can pick up something to mark an occasion, I feel good."

"February 25. October 3. June 4."

"Excuse me?"

He slapped one of the meatballs onto the counter, then peeled it off and popped it directly onto the built-in grill. "February 25. My birthday. October 3. The anniversary of the Group's incorporation." A second patty hit the counter and went the way of the first. "June 4. My graduation from college. Now *that* was a milestone. It was a miracle I made it, a miracle the university swallowed its pride and presented me my diploma. Not that I saw the graduation exercises myself. I was in the parking lot slipping propaganda leaflets under windshield wipers." Having set two more patties onto the grill, he turned with his fist on his hip and his eyes skyward. "What was it that time? Fraternity discrimination? Fluoridation of the water?" He threw a hand in the air, then held up a finger. "Ah. One more. November 23."

When he offered no significance for the date, Liz eyed him strangely. "The day Kennedy was shot?"

Donovan grew serious, but in a soft and vulnerable way. "The day my son was born."

"Your son? But I thought . . ."

"We never married, Ginny and I. David was a love child. Unfortunately, Ginny and I outgrew our love—and each other—pretty soon after we graduated. It was one of those really quick things. We met, we loved, we parted. She met someone else within a year and got married."

"And . . . David?"

"David got a stepfather who loved him, thank God. Ron adopted him legally, as a matter of fact, and gave him his name. He and Ginny have three other children now, and David's been happy."

"Do you ever see him?"

"More, now that he's older." Wiping his hands on a dish towel, Donovan pulled his wallet from his back pocket and dug out a picture, which he handed to Liz. "It was taken a year ago."

Liz studied the picture for a long time. She could see Donovan's healthy coloring in David's face, as well as the same deep-brown eyes and firm jaw. "He's a handsome boy."

"Almost a man. He'll be seventeen next month."

She looked at the picture for a minute longer before handing it back. "You must be proud of him."

"I am, though I don't really have a right to be. I contributed to his gene composition. That's about it."

"You're his father."

"But I've had little to do with his upbringing."

"Did you want it differently?"

Having returned the picture to its place, Donovan tucked the wallet into his pocket. He drew a spatula from a nearby drawer and tended to the quickly broiling patties. She wondered why he kept his back to her, then understood when he spoke slowly and with an unmistakable note of shame. "At the time, no. I was into doing my own thing—the 'me-generation' personified. But I outgrew that particular self-indulgence, too. And now I'm sorry for all I missed of David's life. He's a super guy. I guess I should be grateful that Ginny and Ron made him that way." He flipped the burgers before turning around. "I don't know why I'm telling you all this."

Liz wasn't at all puzzled. "I'm a good listener."

"I haven't told many people about David. It's ... difficult to admit that I was so irresponsible when I was young."

"You were young. That says it all."

"Ginny was young, too, but she was a wonderful mother."

"She had nine months of practice even before David was born. Besides, if she married soon after graduation and had three more children, she must have wanted that kind of life. She must have been ready for it. You just . . . took a little longer."

He tipped his head. "Why are you so understanding?"

His perplexity brought a gentle smile to Liz's lips. "Because it all makes sense. If you'd forced yourself to settle down then, you'd probably have been miserable. And you might never have been able to achieve what you have since. Besides, I'm looking from the outside in. It's easier to put things in perspective when you're not personally involved."

"Did you ever want kids?"

"I love kids."

"But did you ever want to have your own?"

Did she ever! But it was a dream, nothing more. Seeking a diversion, she focused on the thin tendrils of smoke rising from the Jenn-Air. "I think our lunch is burning."

Whirling around, Donovan rescued the burgers. Within minutes he'd heated buns, melted cheese atop the patties and presented Liz with what truly were the most delicious cheeseburgers she'd ever tasted.

By the next morning, though, she had a case of heartburn that had nothing to do with what she'd eaten.

2

"I THINK VERONICA SHOULD be handling the DIG Group," Liz informed her boss soon after the latter had arrived at the office.

Karen Reynolds set down the coffee she'd been sipping and eyed Liz over the rims of her tortoiseshell spectacles. "Why Veronica?"

"She's been with you longer than I have. She's more experienced."

"You're brighter."

"Then . . . maybe Julie. She's *brilliant*."

"Julie has her hands filled with the book tour for Jonathan Douglass."

"I've got my hands filled, too. There's publicity to be arranged for Eastern Leather and the quarterly report to be done for Humbart, and I've got to set up meetings with the media to stir up interest in the *Women's Journal*. . . ."

Karen's brows met as she studied Liz's agitated state. "What's wrong, Liz? What happened yesterday?"

Liz began to pace across the plush mauve carpet. "I met with him. We talked. I just think that I'm the wrong person to be working on this case."

"You're my troubleshooter. You're the *best* one for this case."

Liz stopped in front of the desk, her worried eyes suddenly brightening. "How about Donna? She's as much of a troubleshooter as I am."

"Donna's got a husband and two kids and her hours are more limited. Besides, I want *you*. Damn it, Liz. Don't start pacing on me again. Sit down and tell me what the problem is."

Liz sent her a frustrated glance from midway across the room. "The problem is Donovan Grant."

"Donovan a *problem*? I don't believe it. He was always the most easygoing, nicest guy."

"I don't think I can work with him."

Karen settled back in her chair, clearly perplexed. "I thought you two would hit it off well." Indeed that was what she'd intended, for more than business reasons. She wasn't usually a matchmaker, but somehow the image of Donovan and Liz together had struck an instant chord in her. "What happened?"

"He's a tease."

"*Donovan Grant*? Are you sure we're talking about the same man? The Donovan I knew was soft-spoken and earnest. A tease? No. Charming maybe." She grinned. "And gorgeous without a doubt." She shook her head, then paused with a hint of that same innocent curiosity Donovan had shown when he and Liz had discussed Karen. "What does he look like now?"

For the first time that day, Liz smiled. "He wondered about you, too."

"It's been better than seventeen years since I've seen him—other than grainy photos in magazines. Has he aged well?"

Liz's lips thinned. "I don't think he's aged."

"Come on. Time passes. What does he look like?" When Liz turned to stalk to the far side of the office, Karen rolled her eyes. "Liz, *sit down*." Only after Liz had begrudgingly settled into the nearest chair did she prod. "Well?"

Liz reluctantly met her gaze. "I didn't know him before, but he looks . . . good."

"He always looked good. Come on, Liz. Give."

Liz forced herself to paint with words the picture that had been so vividly in her mind's eye for the past hours. "He's tall and lean but solid. Clear brown eyes. A full head of brown hair with lighter streaks near the temples."

"Grey?" Karen asked with a wide grin. She was thinking of her monthly trips to the colorist and was delighted to know that she wasn't the only one showing telltale signs of middle age. Liz, God bless her, didn't have that problem, and she'd never have tried to cover it up if she did, Karen knew.

"Gray? Uh . . . I'm not sure. Maybe, but he seemed so boyish."

"The man has to be thirty-nine, if not forty. It *has* to be gray."

"Whatever it is, it becomes him. Like the crow's-feet at the corners of his eyes. And the tiny lines on his forehead. And his dimples—"

"His dimples! God, how could I forget those. They always did the weirdest things to my insides."

"Exactly." Liz also recalled the fine sprinkling of dark hair on the back of his hands, the way his Adam's apple bobbed gently when he swallowed, the litheness of his walk that suggested long, firmly corded legs hidden beneath the oh-so-soft denim of his jeans. But she didn't want to tell Karen about those things. She didn't want to think about those things, yet they persisted in haunting her. Even the memory of his voice, warm and soothing, was a balm that grated.

"So, what's the problem?" Karen broke into her thoughts, then grew smug with suspicion when Liz's glazed look registered. "You did discuss the contamination of his fields, didn't you?"

The glazed look vanished, replaced by the professional one Karen was so much more familiar with. "Oh yes. Some of what he said I already knew from the newspapers—that the fields in question are in Southern California and produce lettuce. *Organically grown* lettuce."

"Which means?"

"Lettuce grown on composted soil without manufactured fertilizers, pesticides or herbicides. According to Donovan, the only sprays used on organically grown products are those derived directly from plants such as garlic and nettle. Someone obviously went out of his way to spray something else."

"Does he have any idea who?"

Liz shook her head. "He's as much in the dark about who might have done it as the authorities are. He's been in touch with the families of the two women who died, and he makes daily calls to the hospital in Sacramento where other patients are being watched. It's impossible to know exactly how many people were affected in all; some suffered nothing more than intense cases of indigestion, which worked themselves out in a day. We agreed that the best thing would be for him to go public, discussing the problem and the security measures he's taken to make sure nothing like this happens again."

"Security measures?"

"He's hired guards and is in the process of buying a radar-type detector that can scan his fields and make sure nothing hits them from the air. That's how it was done before—a fine-grain poison dusted over one of the fields at night. No one really noticed a plane buzzing low, and it was foggy besides."

"It was a miracle the plane didn't crash in the fog," Karen mused dryly.

"Whoever did it had guts, that's for sure."

"And there are no leads at all as to who it was?"

Liz shook her head. "Investigators have gone through logs at every airport in the area. It was probably a private plane taking off from a private airstrip. The authorities are hoping for a tip from someone somewhere. Otherwise . . ."

"Otherwise they'll never know."

"Right. From a selfish point of view, it would make matters that much better if the case were solved. Then we could attribute the whole thing to one particular crackpot."

"Is that what Donovan thinks? That it was a crackpot?"

"You mean, rather than someone who specifically had something against him?" Liz countered. "I asked him that, but he says he doesn't have any enemies." She clearly remembered the innocent way he'd said it, and her subsequent chiding. "I suggested that it might have been someone jealous of his success, but he brushed that possibility aside. Anyway, if whoever it was is caught, the situation will be better for all of us."

Karen retrieved her coffee and took a thoughtful sip. "Okay. So you'll go public. I agree that that's the best tack." Realizing that for the moment Liz had forgotten her request to be removed from the case, she eyed her with studied nonchalance. "What, specifically, did you have in mind?"

Liz didn't even see herself as stepping into a trap, because professionalism had taken over and she was drawn into the excitement of plotting a new and challenging case. "There should be letters to stockholders and associates of the DIG Group, of course, and to the distributors and retailers. But the most effective thing would be a barrage of television and radio talk shows and news spots—Donovan would be perfect for that—and large ads in prominent newspapers. At this point the general public is the problem. If fear leads to a boycott of his entire line of health foods—even though all of the contaminated items have already been removed from the shelves—it could cause irreparable damage to the future of the division. It's too early to get concrete figures, but the communication Donovan's had with distributors tells him that sales are definitely off. That's why we have to hit soon and hard."

Karen sat forward. "Go to it then. I assume you can get the background information you need from someone at DIG headquarters. It's not far from here. Did you arrange something with Donovan?"

Did I arrange something with Donovan? The question brought Liz from the professional to the personal with a jolt. Bounding from her seat, she made it to the window before she turned back. "He said he'd be by later to take me over. I thought that you and I could agree on a replacement by then."

"A replacement? But you've barely started. And you've got such good ideas. This case is tailor-made for you."

"I'm going to have trouble, Karen," Liz countered beseechingly.

Karen studied her friend's face, then spoke softly. "Donovan scares you, and it's got nothing to do with business."

Liz dropped her gaze. "I feel uncomfortable with him."

"It's natural to feel a little uncomfortable with a new client."

"Not a little uncomfortable. A *lot* uncomfortable."

"You'll get over it once you start working."

But Liz was shaking her head. "I don't think so."

"Why not?"

"Because . . . because he's so . . . so . . ."

"Good-looking? You've worked with good-looking men before."

"It's not that. He's so . . . so . . ."

"Charming? That'll only make it all the more pleasant."

Again Liz was shaking her head, but she was no closer to finding the word that explained her problem. Sure, she'd worked with good-looking men before, many of whom had been charming, as well. But she'd never felt so threatened. Something in her gut stirred when she thought of Donovan Grant, and it set her on edge.

"I just can't relax with him," she ventured at last, launching an appeal to Karen's business sense. "And if I can't do that, I doubt I'll be able to do the kind of job this firm prides itself on."

Karen wasn't fooled for an instant, but then, just as she was an expert at constructing credible facades, so she could easily see through ones that weren't quite so credible. She knew that Liz had the same aptitude and therefore she had no qualms about calling her bluff. Perhaps bluntness was what was needed. "Tell me something, Liz," she commanded gently. "Do you *like* Donovan? Is that what's worrying you?"

Liz scowled. "Of course not."

"Of course not...what? You don't like him, or that's not what's bothering you?"

Liz sensed she was getting in over her head. "I don't think in terms of *liking* my clients. You know that."

"It wouldn't be so bad . . . with someone like Donovan."

"That doesn't make good business sense."

"I'm not talking business."

Liz sent her an imploring look. "How can you do this to me?"

Pushing herself from her chair, Karen came around the desk to put an arm across Liz's shoulders. "I can do it because I'm your friend. Because I *care* about you. Because I think that at first sight Donovan Grant got under your skin. And because I know what that feeling's like."

"Maybe *you* should be working with him."

Karen laughed, then proceeded to echo Donovan's own thoughts. "I can't give him the attention his case deserves. If there's one thing I've learned in twelve years of building this business, it's to delegate work. Besides, I've had my day with Donovan. We enjoyed each other, then moved on. Donovan's not right for me. He's too . . . too soft. I was always more aggressive than he was, more ambitious."

"How can you say that, looking at the corporation he's built for himself? He has to be aggressive *and* ambitious."

"I know Donovan better than that. He may look a little different now. He may be more sophisticated, more experienced. But he's still sensitive and, from what I've read, he's a pragmatist. I'd dare say that if the DIG Group fell apart tomorrow and there was no possible way it could be retrieved, he'd very calmly turn his sights to something else."

"If that's true, why is he so worried about the damage this poison business will do?"

"Because he's bright. And this is a new challenge to face. Donovan always thrived on new things—new people, new ventures. Why do you think he keeps inventing new divisions for the Group? This year it's Chimera. Next year it'll be something else."

She grew more pensive before speaking again. "It's not that he loses interest in the old things, because I doubt he does and his record doesn't suggest it. He was always dedicated to whatever cause he chose to espouse. Mind you, when we were in school together, he was as carefree as the rest of us. But I always had a feeling about him, about what was lurking behind that carefree front. He's become a very responsible individual." She gave Liz's shoulder a squeeze. "I'd guess it's loyalty to his health-foods business that makes him want to fight to keep it alive."

Liz was thinking about responsibility and what Donovan had said about his son, and wondered if Karen was right in guessing that he'd finally found himself. If so, she admired him for it, though that didn't do anything to ease her own predicament.

"I'd really feel better if you put someone else on his case," she pleaded softly.

"And I think I'd never forgive myself if I did," Karen countered, walking Liz to the door while she was ahead in the game. She knew how her mother must have felt sending her only daughter, crying and pleading, off to overnight camp; once she'd overcome her homesickness, Karen had loved it. As her mother must have done then, so Karen now prayed that she was doing the right thing by sticking to her guns. "Look, just give it a little longer. Get going on the work. If things continue to bother you, we can talk about it again. Just remember that Donovan's a special friend of mine and I *know* that you're the best one for this job."

Liz sent her a look that said she saw right through the flattery, but she also knew that, for the time being at least, the issue was dead. Karen was her boss and, despite their friendship, Liz wasn't about to push her too far. Contrariness wasn't one of Liz's natural traits. Nor was recklessness. Her position at Reynolds Associates meant far too much to her to jeopardize because of one client.

COME LUNCHTIME, though, Liz had second thoughts about that. With a surprisingly productive morning behind her, she was just beginning to feel confident when Donovan appeared at the door of her office and threw her off balance again.

"Hi," he said in that soft, flowing way of his as he stepped into the room. This time it wasn't his balmy voice that disturbed her, or even his smile, which was as brilliant as ever. Rather it was the way he looked. "Uh, is everything all right?" he asked, hesitating at her stricken expression.

For a moment she couldn't reply. He glanced down at himself, then sheepishly met her wide-eyed gaze. "I wanted you to be more comfortable today. This was—is more what you expect, isn't it?"

He wore a three-piece suit of the finest beige wool and looked positively gorgeous. "What I expect?" she echoed dumbly.

"Formality and all?" He ran a finger inside the collar of his shirt, as though he was ill at ease, when in fact Liz could only marvel at the positively masterful way he wore the suit.

"You look fine," she finally managed, at which point he grinned again and, in sheer self-defence, she dropped her gaze to the desk. "What're you doing?" he asked, walking quietly toward her.

"Hmm?"

He cocked his head toward the papers at her fingertips. "Anything good?"

"Uh, a quarterly report for one of our clients."

"Would you rather I come back later?"

"No, no." She quickly gathered the papers into a pile and pushed them aside, then stood. "You're a client, too, and we did have an appointment." She was determined to remember that, despite what Karen had said, he was *only* a client. "Would you like to stop in and say hi to the boss?"

"I already have. It was wonderful seeing her again."

Liz nodded, unsure as to what to say next. Donovan took that responsibility out of her hands in a way that forced her to respond, and quickly.

"You look lovely today." He marveled again at the natural look to her, the faint flush on her cheeks, the guileless lowering of her lids. Then he gave an approving once-over to her plum-hued suit and the matching necktie that bisected the front of her white blouse.

"Shall we go? We've got a lot of ground to cover." She kept her eyes averted, focusing first on the pads of paper and pens she was stuffing into her bag, then on the coat she crossed the room to retrieve from behind the door.

"I thought we'd stop for lunch before we hit the office."

"That's not necessary. I'm sure you've got plenty else to do."

"I've got time for lunch. I'm hungry. Aren't you?"

She ventured a skeptical glance at him. "You're always hungry."

"At mealtimes, yes." He grinned. "See, I'm trying."

"Trying?"

"To watch myself. That comment about hunger could have easily drawn a less innocent response."

Her lips thinned, but there was no anger in her eyes. How could there be when her gaze was filled with Donovan's boyish innocence? "But you've made your point anyway, haven't you?"

"I just want you to know that I'm trying, that I'll *continue* to try not to be offensive."

"You're not offensive."

"But I say things that upset you."

She took a deep breath, then let it out. "I'm just supersensitive, but it's my problem, not yours. You've got a job that needs to be done. I have no problems on that score."

"Then you're saying that if I keep things on a business level we'll be okay?"

"Yes. That's what I was trying to say yesterday."

He paused for an instant, regarding her thoughtfully. Then his expression took on a note of pleading that would have been humorous had she not been particularly susceptible to everything else about him. "Can't we be . . . friends?"

She'd barely begun to search for an answer when her phone rang and, grateful for the diversion, she excused herself softly and turned to answer it.

"Elizabeth Jerome here."

"Liz? It's Cheryl. I think we've got a problem."

Cheryl Obermeyer was the executive vice-president and chief executive officer of her own family's corporation. Encompassing a nationwide chain of discount department stores, it was presently having its share of financial worries. Liz, who'd spearheaded the chain's public-relations efforts for the past five years, was intimately aware of them.

"Uh-oh. Not something with the designer contract?" In an attempt to bolster its image, the chain had recently paid dearly for the right to carry, at a discount, the clothing of an internationally known designer. The bulk of Liz's recent efforts had gone into notifying stockholders, investors and the media of this upgrading of the store's inventory.

"No, thank heavens. This time it's Ray."

"Ray?" Ray Obermeyer was Cheryl's younger brother and a lesser vice-president of the company.

"He's threatening to leave if he's not given more responsibility, and he's making a lot of noise about it."

"Why all of a sudden?"

"He says it's not so sudden, that he's been trying to get more to do for a year. I'm sure it's coming from that bitch of a wife of his—excuse me for saying that, but my sister-in-law has always been a climber. She's probably nagging him about where he'll be in five or ten years and he's getting nervous."

Aware of Donovan standing close behind her, Liz spoke quietly into the phone. "Isn't this something for your father to handle?"

"He's tried, but he's getting nowhere and I'm worried because he doesn't need the strain. He's already had one heart attack. It's bad enough that Ray seems to bungle whatever he's given, but now that he's asking—no, demanding—more, he's really putting Dad on the spot. Me, too, for that matter. I'm the one who's supposed to be running the show."

"Ray knows that and it probably eats at him."

"But what am I supposed to do about it, Liz?" Cheryl asked imploringly. "I can't give him more responsibility if he can't handle what he's already got, and if I don't and he walks out on us, he'll take the image of the family operation right along with him."

Liz fully understood the problem. She'd been behind the image of the family operation from the start. She also empathized with Cheryl and her father, both of whom she'd grown very close to in the past years.

"Maybe it's time to start rethinking the family approach," she suggested softly, but Cheryl's resistance was immediate.

"Not yet. Not until we've tried to work all this out. There's got to be some way of calming Ray down. That's why I'm calling."

Liz waited for the other shoe to fall. She cast an apologetic glance over her shoulder at Donovan, but when he seemed engrossed in a survey of her office, she returned her attention to the phone. "Yes?"

"If you could speak to Ray—"

"Me? But it's a family matter, Cheryl."

"But you've been so close to all of us, and you're so diplomatic. I'm sure Ray would listen to you."

Liz wasn't so sure. From the start she'd sensed something brewing beneath Ray Obermeyer's relatively amiable exterior, and though she knew that he liked her, she was wary. "I could do more harm than good. If he feels that I'm sticking my nose in where it doesn't belong, it could demolish the rapport we've had."

"If he walks out, that rapport would be gone anyway," was Cheryl's pointed response.

"But I'm in no position—"

"You're familiar with the company and with all of us. And you're good, Liz. You're soft-spoken and tactful and intelligent. If you were to suggest to Ray that he'd do well to shine with what he's already got, he'd listen. He respects you. You could tell him that he'll be getting more as time goes on, but that for now the responsibility he's got is plenty. Appeal to his ego. Tell him that he's needed right where he is, that there's no one else who can fill his shoes right now."

"*You're* the one with all the arguments. Why can't *you* make them?"

"Because I'm his sister and coincidentally the CEO of this company. I could say the words and they'd sound either condescending or patronizing. From you, they'd sound like common sense."

Liz closed her eyes for a minute. When she opened them, she caught sight of movement reflected in the brass pen set on her desk. "Listen, Cheryl, can we talk more about this later?"

"I'm leaving for L.A. this afternoon. I won't be back till the beginning of next week. Please, Liz? Will you do it? You'll have the perfect opportunity to talk with him while I'm out of the picture."

"I don't know, Cheryl. It's really not my place."

"As a friend, Liz? That's how I see you and that's why I've called. Will you do me this one favor?"

This last argument was more potent than any that had come before, because Liz was a sucker for friendship and she knew it. "Dirty play, Cheryl."

"I know. But will you?"

Liz sighed. "All right. I'll give it a shot. But I can't promise results. This isn't my usual line of work."

"That's baloney. It's what you do best—dealing with people, making them see varied aspects of a picture. He'll listen to you. I know he will. I'll give you a call when I get back. Maybe we can meet for lunch. Okay?"

That sounds good," Liz said with a smile. She did enjoy Cheryl and the occasional lunches they shared. As for her brother, well, she'd simply have to try her best.

Replacing the receiver in its cradle, she turned back to Donovan. "Sorry about that. She's going out of town and I couldn't get her off the phone."

Donovan didn't seem any the worse for his wait. "Everything okay?"

"I hope so."

"A client?"

"And friend." She rolled her eyes. "There's the catch." Then she abruptly narrowed her gaze on Donovan. "See? That's what I've been trying to tell you. It's a mistake to mix business with pleasure."

"Is it a mistake to have friends?"

"Of course not. But—"

"And if those friends just happen to be people you meet through your work?"

"In theory, it's fine. But—"

"That woman—Cheryl? Do you value her friendship?"

"Of course, but—"

"And if you hadn't happened to work for her, you'd never have met her." He grinned and reached to take her coat from her. "So there's hope for us after all."

Struggling to find further words of protest, Liz turned her back and slid her arms into the sleeves that were deftly offered. But before she could turn back, Donovan's hands settled on her shoulders. His long body was suddenly close, his breath fanning the dark hair by her ear.

"Friends?" was all he said, but it was the way he said it, softly and gently, that would have been her undoing if his nearness hadn't already set her insides to quivering.

Dumbly she nodded, unable to muster a sound as he confidently took her elbow and escorted her from her office. By the time they'd reached the street and the cool October air had revived her somewhat, she'd realized that she couldn't very well turn down his offer. In the first place, it would have been rude to do so; he was a new client, a good friend of Karen's and not to be offended. In the second place, she *did* value friendship. And if that was indeed all he wanted, she stood to benefit from the arrangement. Donovan Grant was interesting and companionable. As for his ability to pierce her soul with a glance, to make her insides stir by dint of his mere presence, well, that was something she was simply going to have to learn to control.

Sliding his palm down her arm, Donovan took her hand and began to walk. "You don't mind, do you? Walking, that is? It's not far to my office and there's a super restaurant along the way."

"I don't mind walking," she said quietly. She made no effort to remove her hand from his. His touch imbued her with a sense of protection, one she'd never missed in the past but which was as pleasant a momentary indulgence as any. "It's a beautiful day. I'm used to walking."

He looked down at her, catching her gaze when it flicked toward his. "That's right. You walk to and from work. Don't you ever get worried in the dark? New York's not the safest city in the world."

"No one notices me. I'm perfectly safe."

"You're a pretty woman in a concrete jungle. I'd say you stand out." When he tipped his head to study her, she tore her gaze away and looked straight ahead. "Of course, you don't wear flashy jewelry. No diamonds or gold chains just begging to be grabbed. Why the scowl?"

"What scowl?"

"The one you're wearing. Listen, it's okay. I'm not big on jewelry myself, either."

Her scowl had nothing to do with jewelry, but she didn't care to enlighten him on that score. Rather, she lifted his hand, their fingers still entwined, and glanced curiously at what little bit of cuff peered from the end of his jacket. Her hunch confirmed, she sent him a pointed look before returning her eyes to the street.

"Okay, okay, so my cuff links are gold. But they were a present from my mother on my sixteenth birthday and I needed *something* to keep these damned cuffs together."

Liz grinned in spite of herself. "Your sixteenth birthday? We're talking history here. Your mother must have been a seer."

"More like a dreamer, at least for a time. She'd just about given up hope on me ever making anything of my life."

"But now you have, and she must be in seventh heaven."

"Not seventh. Just heaven."

Liz caught her breath at her own stupidity. "Hey, Donovan, I'm sorry."

"So am I," he said with a rueful smile. "She deserved some kind of reward after the hell I put her through when I was younger. I wish I could have done something to make it all up to her—not that she needed money. My dad did well. He still does. He's an orthopedic surgeon."

"Really? Where?"

"St. Louis."

"That's where you grew up?"

"Yup." He smoothly steered her around a threesome walking at a snail's pace ahead of them.

"Do you have brothers or sisters?"

"One of each. They're both super achievers, always were. Rather than compete with them, I decided to be different." He chuckled as he guided her around a corner. "Looks like I blew it."

"Does that bother you? I mean, it can't be a matter of competition at this point." She slipped past the door Donovan held and entered the restaurant. He was quickly by her side again.

"It's not, and, no, it doesn't bother me. We're in different fields—my sister's a doctor like Dad and my brother's in real estate. They kinda get a kick out of my showing up for family events wearing peasant pants and a dashiki."

"You don't," Liz chided in response to his mischievous grin.

"Well, maybe only once in a while. Just to remind them I'm me."

"I can't picture *anyone* not knowing you're you."

"If that's a compliment, I thank you." The smile he bestowed upon her was heart-stopping, and for an instant Liz couldn't look away. "Would you like me to check your coat?"

"My coat?" Abruptly she looked down at the simple topcoat, then, with a blush, corralled her senses to obedience. "Uh, no, it's okay. I'll keep it with me."

"For protection?" he teased.

"For warmth," she replied. "I've been here before. The management spares nothing when it comes to air conditioning, even in October."

Donovan's eyes clouded and, three-piece suit and all, he seemed suddenly uncertain. "Would you rather go elsewhere?" he asked quickly.

As had happened before, Liz found his unsureness endearing. It was only second nature for her to reassure him with a gentle smile. "This is fine. And the food's great here."

"Ah." Buoyant once more, he held two fingers up to the hostess and put his hand lightly to Liz's back to guide her through the crowd when they were gestured onward. He stayed close by her side as they walked to the small corner table, drew her chair out and seated her before dropping into his own chair and pulling it close to the table. Then he leaned forward with his forearms straddling his plate and simply grinned.

Discomfited by his obviously undivided attention, Liz dragged her gaze from his and scanned the room. "They always get a good lunch crowd here."

"You come often?"

"Not really. But the few times I have it's been packed. I'm actually surprised we were seated so quickly. Those others waiting must have needed bigger tables."

"I paid the hostess off."

"You what? I didn't see—"

"I stopped in on my way to your office and, uh, reserved a table."

"But they don't take reservations—"

"Anyone takes reservations with the proper incentive. I didn't care to stand around in a crowd. I wanted you all to myself."

"Donovan, you promised . . ." But he was still grinning and she sensed that it was futile to try to argue. Besides, his grin was contagious. "You look like a Cheshire cat. Are you always this way?"

"Nope."

"Then something must be up. Tell me the police have a lead on the mad poison duster."

"If only."

"Oh. By the way, Karen agreed with everything we discussed yesterday."

"I know. Not that it would have mattered. You're the one who's handling my case, and if you and I agree on a course of action, that's all that counts."

"Still, it's nice to have the reassurance."

"I don't need it. I trust you. Do you trust me?"

She looked him in the eye. "No."

"Mmm. That's what I thought." He sighed and sat straighter, but his grin persisted. "Well, that's something I'll have to work on."

When he continued to look at her, Liz made a ceremony of studying her menu. "Do you know what you want?"

He didn't even glance at the selection printed. "Uh-huh."

She looked up sharply, sure she'd caught a hint of suggestiveness in his drawl, but when she would have glared at him in punishment, he spoke quickly.

"The croissant club."

Her hackles settled down. "So you've eaten here before, too?"

"Yup. But I'm sure you weren't here. I would have noticed."

"Donovan..." she warned.

"What are you having?"

She stared at him a minute longer, then looked down at her menu. "I thought I'd have the quiche of the day."

"Without knowing what it is?"

"I like surprises."

"What if it's got spinach in it?"

"I like spinach."

"What about capers?"

She pondered that thought. "I've never had a quiche with capers in it. It'd be interesting."

"Then you are adventurous?"

"I ate your cheeseburgers, didn't I?"

"I like your eyes. Especially when they twinkle like that...oops, there it goes. Hey, don't glare. I didn't mean any harm. I *do* like your eyes."

What Liz was thinking was that she liked Donovan's eyes, too—so clear and chocolaty—and she wished she didn't. His eyes could see so much. Certainly they could see the beautiful blonde at the next table or the stunning brunette at the table beyond that. And here she sat, with straight brown hair, nondescript features and a figure as plain as the rest of her. Donovan's attentiveness had to be a sham. Not for the first time she felt she was being played with. And Donovan seemed so sincere about it that if she didn't watch herself, she'd begin to believe that he *did* like her eyes.

Just then the waitress arrived and Donovan quietly ordered for them both. When they were alone once again, he relaxed back in his chair, though his gaze remained every bit as direct. "So, where do we start this afternoon?"

Liz, too, relaxed. "I'd like to learn as much as possible about the DIG Group. Any written material you can give me would be a help, as would talking with your ad people."

"Are you surprised that I've gone over their heads to hire you to handle this problem?"

"No. It happens all the time. Advertising and public relations may not be mutually exclusive, but they are separate fields. For one thing, my contacts are different from those of your ad department. For another, I don't approach a member of the financial press and try to buy space in his column; that would defeat our purpose and lessen the legitimacy of our case. Oh, and I'd like to meet with your sales and marketing people."

"I can arrange that. Then what?"

"Then I digest it all and come up with a specific plan of attack. It would be great if I could take a look at the media coverage you've had in the past—newspaper and magazine kind of thing."

"Sure. It's all been pretty straightforward, though. We never went looking for publicity because our products and services have sold themselves, which is one of the reasons our ad department is small. This is the first time we've had to specifically think about PR. When I first spoke with Karen on the phone the other day, she mentioned several of the other crisis cases you've handled. Do you thrive in crises?"

"Thrive? I wouldn't necessarily say that. There is an added excitement in crisis cases, as you call them, purely because of the immediacy of the situation. Do you remember the accident in one of the Driscoll hotels several years back, where fourteen people were killed when the roof of the restaurant caved in?"

When he nodded, she went on. "Immediately after the accident there was a deluge of cancellations that threatened to cripple the entire hotel chain. The Driscoll people hired us, and it was nonstop work for a month. We sent letters of reassurance to anyone and everyone involved or planning to be involved with the hotels. We hit the media—much as we'll do with you—and focused directly on the cause of the accident and the subsequent safety checks that had been made on all of the hotels in the chain. Basically, we were able to stem, then turn around the kind of mindless panic that the accident caused."

"The campaign was a success."

"Very much so. We saw results almost instantly, which was rewarding and therefore exciting. Actually, though, noncrisis cases are probably harder to handle."

"In what sense?"

"You've often got to make something out of nothing. In your case, for example, we're starting with a newsworthy event, so that when I approach the media they'll jump at the opportunity to interview you. In the case of, say, an educational-publishing house that may want to push one or another of its publications, you have to really *work* to drum up public interest. Then again there are corporate quarterly reports such as the one I was working on this morning. It's sometimes nearly impossible to come up with the slightly unusual that will catch the eye of the thousands of stockholders who would otherwise throw the thing into the trash. We can spend weeks brainstorming in-house before we finally hit on the tack we want."

"Is Karen's organization a tight-knit one?"

"You mean, do we work together? Yes. That's the beauty of it. Some PR firms in New York have upward of two hundred employees, each assigned to a particular division, whereas there are only twenty of us at Reynolds Associates. We meet as a firm once a week, in smaller groups more often. We get to interact on different accounts and therefore get exposure to many different kinds of cases."

"And you're all women."

Liz grinned. "Each and every one of us."

"Was that a drawing card for you?"

She paused for a minute, wondering whether Donovan implied criticism in his question. As though sensing her wariness, he ventured a smile. "Hey, it's okay. The makeup of Karen's firm certainly didn't deter me. To the contrary. I respect women. They've got creative minds and they're often far more organized than men are. I was just curious about your own feelings."

The problem, Liz realized, was that she *had* been attracted to Reynolds Associates because it was an all-female firm. From the very start of her interviewing process she'd felt more comfortable there than she had at some of the other places at which she'd applied. Unfortunately, she didn't want to have to explain the reason for it to Donovan.

"Karen and I hit it off from the first. I admire her for what she's built, and I share her views on public relations. What with the client list she had even then, I couldn't have refused her offer."

"You haven't answered my question." This time it was Donovan's eyes that twinkled.

But Liz wasn't about to answer his question. "We've had some pretty funny experiences with men, actually. There was one fellow who went from office to office looking for the 'associates.' All he could see were 'secretaries.' Then there was the time we were hired to do a publicity campaign for an underwear manufacturing company and four of us showed up in its boardroom to hear a team of men stammer and sputter about one style of jockey short or another. You see, we don't advertise the fact that there aren't any men in the firm. It's really flattering when men hire us without realizing what they've done."

"But you do the job."

"You bet. How did *you* know we were all women?"

"I had a hunch, knowing Karen. She was a libber even way back then. I think that was one of the reasons we didn't work out as a twosome."

"You don't believe in women's lib?"

"Oh, I believe in it. I just think it goes too far. Too many women seem to have sacrificed the softer side of themselves for the sake of professional advancement."

"Ah. In your old age you'd kind of like to have a woman at home waiting for you, all dolled up and counting the minutes until you step through the door?" she teased.

But Donovan was very serious. "Not at all. I wouldn't respect a woman who did nothing with her time but wait for me, and very honestly, I wouldn't want that kind of responsibility."

"Then what would you want?"

"A woman who had a career but who realized that it wasn't the be-all and end-all of life. A woman who prized her quiet times with me as much as her hectic ones at the office. A woman who was willing to share the responsibilities of a home and family and thereby enable both of us to do more and have more than either of us could do or have alone."

Liz felt her throat grow tight for an instant. What he suggested sounded forbidden yet marvelous. She wondered at the pang of yearning that had momentarily stolen through her iron guard and quickly strove to squelch it. "You're an idealist, Donovan. What you say sounds fine in theory, but statistics have shown that it's the woman who usually ends up shouldering the larger share."

"I cook. I do laundry. Okay, so I hire someone to do the cleaning. But I've lived alone long enough to know that I want more from life than a dark and empty house. Maybe I am a dreamer." He sighed. "God knows I haven't been able to find a woman who fits my qualifications." His expression grew suddenly softer, more vulnerable, and his gaze fell to her lips. "Would you, Elizabeth?"

"Would I what?"

"Be willing to share my dark and empty house?"

3

For a minute Liz could scarcely breathe because her imagination was running away with her. She could have sworn she was being kissed; Donovan's eyes silently but thoroughly savored her lips. She could have sworn he was making a proposal.

But she knew better. She knew that she couldn't begin to compare in either looks or experience with most of the women in the restaurant, certainly not with the women who had to have previously passed through Donovan's life. She knew that Donovan liked to tease, and that he knew she was susceptible to it. Moreover, she knew she wouldn't ever have what he, albeit hypothetically, dangled before her eyes.

Corralling her senses, she wrinkled up her nose and played along. "I hate dark and empty houses."

His gaze slid from her lips to her eyes and was every bit as embracing. "It wouldn't be dark and empty if we were sharing it."

"But I already have a place to live," she countered with respectable serenity.

"You could move."

"I've got a two-year lease."

"I could get you out of it."

"I don't want to get out of it."

"Then ... you're not the kind of woman I'm looking for?"

She rolled her eyes and sighed, feeling in touch with reality once more. "Ah. I'm finally getting through."

His brows met for an instant. "Why did I think you might be?"

"Don't ask me. I've never understood the male mind."

"Never? Wasn't there ever a special man in your life?"

"No."

"Why not?"

"Because I've been busy building a career."

"So you *are* one of them?" A hint of teasing had returned to his voice and Liz was relieved. She was also proud of herself. She'd dealt with Donovan in a calm, sensible manner. This time, for once, she hadn't let his teasing get to her.

"I suppose you could say so," she responded, then smiled graciously as the waitress set her quiche before her.

As though a prime hurdle had been cleared, the rest of their lunchtime passed without a hitch. Donovan made easy conversation, talking of other restaurants he liked, about a show he'd seen the week before that coincidentally she'd seen, too, about skiing prospects for the upcoming winter season. Though Liz didn't ski, she smiled and nodded when he suggested he'd teach her how. Perhaps he'd been right, she mused, when he'd suggested that if she learned to take his teasing in stride she'd discover what a nice guy he was. She *did* like him. Moreover, she felt good being with him. In her eyes he was the best-looking man in the entire restaurant. He didn't glance around to take stock of the other diners. He didn't yawn or look bored when she talked. He was attentive and interested. She couldn't have asked for a more pleasant client.

When they finished lunch he walked her to his office. He didn't hold her hand this time and although one tiny part of her missed the warmth of his strong fingers, the larger part felt she'd scored a victory for detachment.

Negotiating the afternoon foot traffic with ease, he maintained a running commentary on the history of the DIG Group and its installation in the Park Avenue office toward which he guided her. After the elevator had carried them to a floor high above the city street and deposited them in an attractive reception area, he led her from office to office, introducing her to his employees.

Donovan was well liked by his staff. Liz could see it in the smiles that lit faces when he appeared, in the respect, clearly neither obligatory nor reluctant, which greeted his introduction of her. He paved the way and she was welcomed warmly. She felt mildly bereft when he deposited her with the head of his sales department and took his leave, but she was soon engrossed in discussion and busily taking notes.

From sales she was shuttled to marketing, then to advertising. Somewhere along the way a conference room was put at her disposal, and when her meetings were done she found there, as promised, a stack of printed matter for her study.

In the course of the afternoon she learned that, in addition to those endeavors she already knew about, the DIG Group had divisions that sold running and outdoor gear as well as spa equipment. As if that weren't enough to keep one Donovan Grant occupied, she learned that even beyond the consulting he did, he regularly ran management-training sessions for upper-echelon employees of companies from coast to coast.

As he'd suggested, the publicity the Group had hitherto received had been straightforward. Indeed it was positive overall, even glowing on occasion, but in no instance did it appear that Donovan had personally capitalized on the attention.

His modesty suited Liz's purposes beautifully. The fact that he'd kept a low profile in the past would be an asset when she approached the media. His would be a fresh face, a new voice. And he'd go over famously.

"You're looking very pleased with yourself," came that "new" voice, which wasn't new at all but by now hauntingly familiar to Liz.

Her eyes shot toward the doorway in which Donovan leaned, and her pulse quickened. "I didn't realize you were there."

"You seemed totally involved with whatever it is you're smiling about. I take it you like what you've read?"

"I'm impressed." She dropped her gaze to the report she was holding to buy a moment's time in which to compose herself. She desperately wished that her insides would behave, that they wouldn't start jumping each time Donovan was near. "Your organization's well run. Your reputation's well earned."

With a smile, he lazily pushed off from the door-jamb and approached her. "It'd be awful if I didn't practice what I preach."

"I think it's the other way around. You preach what you practice. I hadn't realized you were into sporting gear, as well."

"The motivation for that was selfish. I like sports." He perched on the edge of the table near her. Defensively she sat farther back in her seat.

"Do you run?" she asked.

"Several times a week."

"And I know that you ski."

"I also scuba dive when I can. And go rafting. And sky-dive."

"Ah-hah. You like to tempt the fates." She sounded more cocky than she felt. It was hard, with him so close, with those eyes of his spearing her in such a gentle, if deceptive, way.

"That I do. How about dinner?"

"Dinner?" She glanced at her watch and gasped. "Oh, Lord, I hadn't realized it was so late." She quickly stood and began to gather together the reports she'd been reading.

"It's not late. It's a perfect time for dinner."

"I have to run."

"You run, too?"

"When I'm late," she snapped. "Yes."

He seemed undaunted by her tone, his own softer than ever. "But you haven't given me an answer."

Unable to meet his gaze, she reached for her purse and thrust her notebook inside. "I thought I had. I've got to be going."

"You have plans for the evening?"

"Yes."

"A date?"

"No." She was about to lift the stack of reports when Donovan's hand caught her wrist.

"You don't have to work at night," he said soberly. "Not for me, at least."

Her gaze settled on his fingers and she swallowed. "I wasn't planning to work."

"Then what?" He raised his other hand to her arm and began to lightly, lightly stroke it from elbow to shoulder.

Liz wanted to step away, but she couldn't. As gently as he held her, she felt totally immobilized. "Don't," she whispered. Something had slipped beyond her control and she was frightened.

"What do you have to do tonight?"

She focused on his shirtfront, which didn't help her much because it looked so soft and she could all but see the warm flesh beneath.

"I've got to baby-sit."

"Baby-sit? You're moonlighting?"

"It's for a friend."

He tipped her chin up with his forefinger and she was forced to meet his gaze. "For a friend."

"Yes," she whispered. Further sound seemed beyond her. She shrank into herself but couldn't go far because Donovan's free arm was around her waist, drawing her forward almost imperceptibly.

His eyes skimmed each of her features, soothing her, ruffling her. She tried to steady her breathing, which had suddenly grown shallow and quick, and she was sure he saw the agitated rise and fall of her chest though his eyes didn't venture that low.

"And you don't have time for a quick bite on the way?" His voice was a whisper now, too, though rather than being fearful as hers had been it was tinged with hoarseness and infinitely seductive.

She shook her head, then swallowed convulsively when he dipped his head and feather-touched her cheek with his mouth. "Don't," she whispered again, but she couldn't turn her head, couldn't free herself from his grasp, couldn't run. His lips moved higher and she shut her eyes. The warmth of his body incited her, his clean male smell entranced her. She was helpless to resist the ghostlike kisses he rained slowly over her face. They were soft and beckoning, tempting her with something she'd never in her life known before.

A tiny whimper slipped from her throat and she swayed, only to find herself supported in the cradle of his thighs, with his hands splayed across her back. When he raised his head, she opened her eyes and looked up at him.

He said nothing at first, simply continued to explore her features with a slumberous gaze. While his thighs held her, he brought his hands to her shoulders, caressing them, then her collarbone. His palms slid over the silk of her blouse, making a slithering sound that reverberated through her body.

"You're very soft," he murmured.

She shook her head, but slowly this time. The heels of his hands were perilously close to her breasts, which to her dismay tingled and swelled. She felt awakened, and scared.

"I knew it would be this way."

"What way?"

"My burning, your melting."

"It's not."

"But you're trembling."

"You're frightening me."

"No. You're frightening yourself, and needlessly."

"I'm . . . not."

His hands continued their slow torment and she brought her own up to press them still. It didn't occur to her that she was holding him closer, but he wasn't as naive as she was.

"It's inevitable, Elizabeth," he whispered. "Why do you fight it?"

"Nothing's inevitable," she answered painfully.

"This is. We affect each other. My heart's beating as fast as yours is." As though her hand weighed no more than thistledown, he moved his own beneath it to cover her breast. She sucked in a breath and bit her lip, afraid that she'd make a sound to belie what she knew she had to say.

"I told you. You're scaring me. I don't like your kind of play"

"Is that why your breasts are fuller? You're responding to me."

"No . . ."

"There's nothing wrong with it, love. It's beautiful. Even when I touch you here . . ." His thumb grazed her nipple and a flare of electricity shot through her. The newness of it, its mind-blowing force gave her the strength to push back from him, but his thighs only tightened to keep her close. "I'd never hurt you. Is that what's got you scared?"

She was breathing heavily, her chin tucked to her chest. Even with his hands safely removed to her waist, she felt threatened. "I don't want this."

"You want to baby-sit."

She nodded.

"Then kiss me and I'll let you go."

"No."

"Aren't you curious? I haven't kissed you yet."

"Yes, you did. Before."

"Not on your lips. Not with you responding that way."

She shook her head in denial of his request, but again he forced her head up. "I'm not letting you go until you do."

"Please don't do this to me," she begged. "Play your games with someone who can handle them."

"I think you can handle them just fine. That's why I'm challenging you."

"But I don't *want* to play."

"One kiss."

She pressed her lips together.

"You're chicken."

She nodded.

"Come on, Elizabeth."

"It's *Liz*," she cried, having had just about enough of his seductive tone. "Everybody calls me *Liz*."

"I'm not everybody. I'll call you Elizabeth."

She closed her eyes and moaned, but the sound was barely half out when it was swallowed by Donovan's mouth. With a muted groan of protest, she tried to push him away, but his fingers were suddenly tangled in her hair, holding her head so that she couldn't escape his lips.

Later, Liz was to analyze that kiss, from its first unrelenting claim, through its gradual softening, to its final devastating persuasiveness. She'd remember the way his mouth had slanted over hers, firmly and possessively, then with finesse and a tempered hunger. She'd remember the way his tongue had stroked hers, challenging it, calling it from hiding, tempting it, finally mating so fully with it. She'd remember the way his teeth had nibbled on her lips, the way his breath had mingled with hers. And she'd be shocked that she'd allowed herself this cruel glimpse of paradise.

For now, though, she could only go with the flow, too weakened to fight, too inflamed to resist. When he finally set her back, her cheeks were hot and her entire body throbbed.

"There," he said with a satisfied grin, "*now* we can go."

Ignoring the "we" and the way her limbs quaked, she reached for the reports, but he lifted them first and balanced them in one arm. With the other he took her coat from the chair and held it while she put it on. When she'd thrust her pocketbook strap over her shoulder, she held her arms out for the reports.

"I'll carry them down and get you a cab."

"That won't be necessary."

"Still, I'll do it."

Determined only on escaping this room, this building, this man, Liz stormed ahead. She didn't look at him once during the wait for the elevator or the purring ride

down, and she hailed her own cab, though in other cir-
cumstances she would have walked. Only after she'd
somewhat ungraciously flounced into the cab did she
hold out her arms for the reports. Not relinquishing
them yet, Donovan bent low.

"I'm off to New Orleans tomorrow morning but I'll
be back the next day. I'll call you then. Okay?"

"Fine," she gritted. "I'll pass these reports and my
notes on to whomever will be taking over your case."

"You'll be handling it."

"No way."

"It's either you or no one."

She stared at him angrily. "You mean that you'd actually go to another firm if you don't get your way?"

"Yes."

"That's childish."

"See? We're alike that way, too."

Before Liz could think of a suitably cutting remark,
he'd deposited the reports in her lap, closed the door
and given it two taps in indication that the cabbie
should move. Which he did.

"I'M SORRY, KAREN, but I've tried and it won't work.
You're going to *have* to put someone else on Donovan
Grant's case."

Karen had been waiting for Liz's visit, well prepared
for agitation this time. "Donovan told me you wanted
out."

"He *told* you?"

"He called me last night. We had quite a talk."

"Did he tell you that he attacked me?"

"That . . . wasn't exactly the word he used."

Liz felt mortification begin to mix with her annoyance, because she half suspected that Donovan had told Karen exactly what he'd done. "What did he say?" she asked more timidly. She had to know exactly how far the man would go.

Karen shrugged. "He said that he'd kissed you and that you hadn't liked it."

"That was very perceptive of him."

"He said you were frightened."

"You bet I was. Social rape isn't any more pleasant than the other kind."

"Do you know about . . . the other kind?"

Liz looked at her sharply, then relaxed slightly when she saw that Karen was both curious and genuinely concerned. "No. I've never been raped."

"I was wondering."

"You mean, because I seem so resistant to Donovan?"

"Actually, I was thinking about men in general," Karen went on gently. "In the six years I've known you, you haven't dated any man more than once or twice, and even then the dates have been few and far between. When I've tried to fix you up, you've refused. I . . . it's only natural that I'd wonder . . ."

"Well, you don't have to," Liz murmured grudgingly. "Men don't enthrall me. That's all. I don't see that my life is missing anything without them."

"What you don't know, you can't miss."

"That works both ways. And why should I ask for trouble?"

"There doesn't have to be trouble."

Liz eased into a chair and folded her hands in her lap. "Okay, Karen. Why haven't *you* settled down?"

"I have settled down. With this business. I don't need the burden of a husband or children. But I wasn't talking about settling down. I was talking about dating. I do plenty of that. And I enjoy it. There are some things men are good for."

The tiny tilt in Karen's lips spoke volumes. Liz eyed her skeptically. "You don't sleep around, Karen. I know you haven't been seeing anyone but David Brewer for the past six months."

Karen gave a small toss of her head, both acknowledging Liz's statement and shrugging it off at the same time. "David happens to do it very well. And he's not demanding or bothersome. He knows that if he talks marriage I'll be gone. But...I'm not the issue here. You are."

Liz sighed wearily. Karen couldn't know that she'd spent her night pacing the floor, but she certainly felt it herself. Her muscles were tense, she'd already taken three aspirin for her headache, and the abundant caffeine she'd consumed this morning had done nothing for her edginess. "I just want off this case. Karen, I've never asked anything like this before, and I know that I may be jeopardizing our relationship. Donovan was—is—a good friend of yours. And I apologize. But I just can't work with him."

"He said he wanted you."

"Or no one? Umm. That's what he told me."

"He said he'd take his case to another firm," Karen stated calmly.

"He's bluffing. He loves games, and this is game playing to the hilt."

"You sound sure that he won't do it."

"I am. The first time I met him he told me that he chose our firm because he felt it was the best. Going to the best is part of his economic philosophy. Listen, Donovan's out of town now for at least a day. If you were to reassign the case, whoever takes over will have time to talk with me, to study my notes, to read the papers and reports I got at his office yesterday. The transfer can be a fait accompli by the time Donovan returns, and once he gets a look at either Veronica or Julie or... or Brenda or Sheila, he'll forget me in an instant."

"I doubt that," Karen began, only to be interrupted when her secretary rushed in with a pained look on her face.

"I told him he'd have to wait, but he insisted." She darted nervous glances from Liz to Karen and back, and Liz's eyes widened, expecting Donovan's momentary entrance. But another man stepped into view. He was younger, tall and rather gangly, with shaggy brown hair that accentuated his pallor.

Liz was on her feet in an instant. "Jamie! What are *you* doing here?"

"I had to see you, Liz." He looked briefly at Karen, but seemed more annoyed than penitent. "We have to talk."

It had been over six months since Liz had seen Jamie, and she was taken totally off guard by his sudden appearance, particularly since he lived better than twenty-five hundred miles away. "Uh, sure. Jamie . . . uh, Karen, this is my kid brother. Jamie, Karen Reynolds, my boss."

If she'd put the "kid" on as a way of telling Karen that Jamie was to be excused for his behavior, it seemed to have worked, because Karen nodded and smiled warmly. Conversely, if Liz had added "my boss" as a means of conveying a message to Jamie Jerome, it fell flat. Jamie nodded once in Karen's direction, but his attention was quickly back on Liz.

"Can we go somewhere?" he asked tersely.

"Uh, sure." Clutching her hands together, she looked at Karen. "We'll finish this discussion later?" she asked softly.

Karen gave a quick nod of understanding and waved her hand, gesturing the two Jeromes out the door. Liz waited until they were in the hall and walking at a fast clip toward her office before she looked up at her brother and spoke.

"What's wrong?"

"What isn't?"

"Has something happened?"

"You could say that. Where's your office?"

"Right up ahead." Without trying to draw anything further from him, she led him past the few remaining doors to her own, then closed it quietly when he'd entered and thrown himself into the nearest chair. "Okay, Jamie," she said gently. "Nice and slow. What's brought you to New York?"

"I'm in trouble."

It was nothing new, though Liz had hoped that with maturity and the professional help he was receiving Jamie would have begun to gain greater control over his impulses. "What is it?" She might have added "this time," had it not been for the personal responsibility she felt.

"I've been going with this girl—"

"Anne?"

"No. Another one. Her name's Susan. We got into a fight and, well, I guess I hit her."

Liz closed her eyes for a pain-filled minute, then opened them and slowly stepped over Jamie's sprawled legs and made her way to the other chair. She needed to sit down. This day had been rotten from the start and was promising to get no better.

She eased herself down and took a shaky breath. "You hit her. Is that it?"

"Well, I guess I did it a couple of times."

"How badly was she hurt?"

"Not terribly."

"Did she have to go to the hospital?"

"Yes."

With a soft moan Liz let her head fall back. "Oh, Jamie," she whispered. "Why?"

"I broke her nose."

"Why did you *hit* her?"

"Because she was taunting me. She was making me feel like a jerk, and I don't have to take that from anyone."

"But to *hit* her...that doesn't accomplish anything."

He gave a grunt. "Now you tell me. She's pressing charges."

Liz bolted forward. "She went to the police?"

"Yes."

"Were you . . . booked?"

"I was on a plane before they could reach me. Susan, dummy that she is, called to tell me they were on their way."

Liz pressed her fingers to her temple, which had begun to throb worse than ever. She knew she had a migraine coming on. She just knew it. "Have you spoken with Dr. Branowitz?"

"No."

"When did you see him last?"

"Last Friday. I was due to see him again tomorrow."

"I think we should call him."

"What good would that do? He's only a shrink, for God's sake, not a miracle worker."

"But he'll know of a lawyer in San Francisco." She leaned toward him. "Jamie, you've got to go back. There's a good chance that you'll get away with probation, especially since you're already under a doctor's care. And you haven't got a record." Which was truly the miracle. Mercifully, the system of justice took no interest in how many different schools a person dropped out of or how many jobs he'd gained and lost.

Jamie simply shrugged. "I don't know. It was getting time to leave anyway. I've been in San Francisco for four years. I think I'd like something new."

"That's just fine, once you settle this thing with Susan."

"She doesn't have to know where I've gone."

"And the warrant that must be out for your arrest? Are you going to let that just . . . hang?"

He shrugged again, but said nothing.

"Jamie," Liz began, trying to be understanding and gentle even as she felt exasperated, "you've got to be realistic. You have a decent job—"

"It's lousy."

"I thought you liked this one. You're with one of the better architectural firms in San Francisco."

"And I'm at the very bottom rung of the ladder. Do you have any idea how distant that top rung looks?"

"Don't worry about the top rung. Worry about the one directly above yours. Rome wasn't built in—"

"Oh, God, spare me!"

"Then *listen* to me, Jamie. You're at the bottom rung of the ladder because you haven't given yourself time enough in any one firm to climb higher. This is the third job you've had in as many years. Okay, so this firm's bigger and more bureaucratic. It might be harder to climb to the top, but at least there should be a handful of people you can get along with."

"They're all snobs."

"They can't be. They hired you."

He'd turned to her, about to argue, when he caught her soft smile. His belligerence faded, and he gave her a begrudging grin. "Yeah. I guess they did."

"Okay. So that's one good thing going for you. Even in spite of the problems you'd had at the other firms, this one saw potential in your work. You've got to give it a chance, Jamie. And San Francisco's a terrific place to be. You've got a good apartment, and then there's Dr. Branowitz."

"For all the good he's doing. Look what happened."

"So you lost control," Liz countered, sounding less concerned than she felt. Losing control to the point of striking out physically was precisely what she'd feared most in Jamie. She didn't want history repeating itself. "But this is the first time...isn't it?" For a minute, when Jamie looked hesitant, Liz felt a sudden chill. "Well, isn't it?"

"Yes."

"Okay. So this is something you can work out with Dr. Branowitz."

"What if I do it again? I didn't mean to hit Susan. I didn't plan it beforehand. It just happened. Maybe I'm just like *him*."

"You're not," Liz snapped, then quickly slipped from her chair to kneel beside her brother. She clasped the hand that lay outspread on his knee. "You're not one bit like Dad," she vowed. "For one thing, you're sensitive and aware and you've got a future ahead of you. For another, you know what it's like to be at the wrong end of a strap and that's pretty awful. For a third, you've got Dr. Branowitz. He's been a help, hasn't he? And you're twenty-five years old. Dad was past forty when he turned on us, and by then he'd just about soured on everything."

"Still, maybe it's in the genes."

"That's a cop-out and you know it, Jamie." She stood, using his knee for leverage, then stared down at him with her jaw hard. "I'm sorry, but I refuse to believe that you're a malicious person. You can go ahead and take the easy way out and blame everything on genes, or a poor role model, or whatever, but it's bull."

"Bull...what?" he teased, evidently bolstered by her pep talk. "Come on, Lizzie. Say it."

"You know what I mean," she snapped crossly.

The roles were suddenly turned and Jamie was the one to be gentle and coaxing, if with a mocking twist. "But it's good to express yourself. Got to get it all out. If you're angry, you need an outlet."

She glared at him, but the corners of her lips were beginning to twitch. "Maybe you've seen *too* much of your doctor friend. Besides, I have an outlet. A headache."

He was serious again. "Hey, I'm sorry. I didn't mean to dump all this on you—"

"You did so. But it's okay. What are big sisters for anyway? And I had the headache before you showed up."

"Bad day."

"You could say that."

"But work's going well . . ."

"Yes, Jamie. Work is going well. I will be able to keep sending you checks. You're paying the doctor on time, aren't you?"

"Sure"

"And the rent? You don't need another eviction notice."

"Naw. I'm all paid up."

She inhaled deeply, then let her breath out slowly. "So. It's only the . . . present problem we have to deal with. How did you get away from the office today? And when *did* you fly in, anyway?"

"I took the red eye last night. And I've got sick time coming. I called one of the other guys before I left and said you were sick."

"*Me?*"

"Yeah. I have to make sure you're okay. After all, you're the only sister I've got."

"How could I forget. Do you think the police will look for you at work?"

Whether or not the thought had occurred to Jamie before, he looked sufficiently disturbed. "Jeez, I hope not."

Liz reached for the phone. "What's Branowitz's number?"

Jamie yawned. "Listen, I'm really exhausted. Jet lag and all. Couldn't we call him later?"

"We'll call him now. At least he can start the ball rolling. It's still early enough there that he might be able to contact the police before they show up at your office . . . if they haven't already. When was it you heard from Susan?"

"When I got home from work yesterday. I might be safe."

Liz sent him a dubious look. "Branowitz's number?" She jotted it down as Jamie recited it, then promptly dialed. Had she been more familiar with psychiatrists, she would have known she'd only reach an answering service. But she wasn't familiar with them, or rather she'd never felt such urgency. Frustrated, she left her number with a message for the doctor to call back. Replacing the receiver, she eyed Jamie again.

"How long does he take?"

He shrugged. "Fifteen minutes. An hour. Six. Who knows? You made it sound like a matter of life and death, so my guess is it'll be sooner rather than later."

"It *is* a matter of life and death—well, figuratively speaking. Jamie, there's an *assault* charge against you.

I mean, if you want to look at the worst of the possibilities, you could go to prison. You'd have a criminal record. And I doubt your firm would take kindly to that."

"The worst won't happen. I knew you'd be able to help. That's why I'm here."

Liz hadn't stopped to wonder why he'd come. She hadn't had to. It wasn't the first time that Jamie had run to her in moments of trial. He'd done it each time he'd dropped out of school, then again when his graduation was threatened at the last minute because of an argument he'd had with one of his professors, then again when he was given his walking papers from the first job he'd had. Though he counted on the money she sent him, she knew that he needed emotional support, as well. She also knew that she'd always be there for him.

"Well," she sighed, walking to her desk. "I guess we just wait for that call."

"I could really use some sleep."

So could I. "Put your head back and rest here. Once we've spoken to Dr. Branowitz you can go over to my place."

It was nearly an hour before the call came through, and during that time, though Liz tried to focus on the quarterly report she'd been working on the morning before, she couldn't involve herself in it. Rather, her mind was on Jamie and his problems. She thought ahead to the possibility of his being incarcerated, and her headache worsened. She knew she'd simply *die* if *she* herself was ever imprisoned. The thought of others having total control of her, of hostile forces being able to make her do whatever they chose, sent terror-filled tremors through her being. And she knew that despite the bravado Jamie showed at times, he'd be terrified, too.

Dr. Branowitz was grateful for her call and thoroughly understanding of the situation. He wondered if a warrant had actually been issued, but agreed to contact the police, as well as a skilled attorney who would represent Jamie. For her part Liz promised to have Jamie on an evening flight back to San Francisco. After giving the doctor her home phone number and extracting a promise that he'd call to report on the progress at his end later in the day, she hung up the phone and dug through her bag for the keys to her apartment. On second thought, she dropped the keys back in her bag and reached for her coat. Much as she loved him, she wasn't sure if she trusted Jamie. If he got to thinking about the things that had shaken *her* in the past hour, he was apt to disappear rather than make that flight to the coast. Far better, she decided, to stay with him until he had safely boarded his plane. She owed it to him. Besides, what was a day off from work? She doubted she'd get much done anyway, given the emotional state she was in. And the throbbing behind her eyes was sheer agony.

Liz left word with her secretary as to where she'd be, then she and Jamie walked home. Though she gently questioned him on what was new in his life, aside from Susan, conversation between them was sparse. As always, Jamie asked few questions himself. Liz had long ago decided that rather than being disinterested, he was simply expressing a kind of confidence that she was fully in command of her life. She was satisfied with that if it made him feel better.

While Jamie slept in her bed, she rested on the sofa. She'd taken more aspirin and had pressed a warm cloth to her eyes. By the time the doctor called back, she felt slightly better, and his news was encouraging. The lawyer, who had agreed to meet with Jamie early the next morning, had already been in touch with the police. It seemed that before a formal complaint could be filed, there would be a preliminary hearing to determine if there was cause for such action. The hearing was set for several days hence, and the lawyer felt confident he could help Jamie.

Liz thanked the doctor profusely, then sagged back into the sofa feeling drained. She tried to sleep, but her mind wouldn't rest. Images of the past rose to haunt her, and she knew she'd get no peace until Jamie was back in San Francisco. Selfish though it might be, she could never live in the same city as her brother. His presence was a reminder of the past and of the responsibility she felt. Oh, she'd always take care of him, send him money, bolster him when he ran to her. But she'd always be relieved when he left. And that compounded her guilt.

Giving up on the idea of sleep, she phoned the airport for Jamie's reservation, then put a beef stew on to cook. Since they hadn't had lunch, she mused, they'd have an early dinner, and there'd be plenty of time to get to the airport afterward.

She was about to wake Jamie when she heard sounds from the shower. A bit later, clean and fresh-shaven, he joined her in the kitchen.

"You need new blades," was the first thing he said. "I used the last one and it was pretty dull."

"And good morning to you."

He was prowling around the small room, seeming unsettled despite his rest. "It's not morning."

"How about some juice?" She started toward the refrigerator, but he waved her away. "Dinner will be ready soon, then," she offered. She waited for him to ask if Dr. Branowitz had called back, but he didn't, so she broached the subject herself. When Jamie took her news with a minimum of enthusiasm, she looked at him in dismay. "I thought you'd be pleased. At least you're not on the verge of arrest."

"You committed me to flying back tonight."

"You have to. You know that."

"I was kind of thinking I'd spend the weekend here. Monday's soon enough to face what's out there."

"Monday's too late. Even Friday's bad enough. You should have been meeting with the lawyer *today—*"

"You don't want me here," he interrupted. There was a sullenness to him that Liz resented, but she'd seen it before and was sure she'd see it again.

"That's not true, Jamie. You know I love you."

"Maybe I cramp your style."

"You do no such thing."

"Maybe you've got a hot date for the weekend."

"Wrong again. I don't go in for 'hot dates.'"

"Ah, I forgot. My sister, the Madonna."

"Why are you doing this to me?" Liz asked, feeling more hurt than anything.

"Doing what?"

"Cutting me down. I don't do it to you."

"And by rights you'd be justified? Is that it?"

"I didn't say that. We're brother and sister, and it looks like we're all we've got. Don't you think it would be better to share a little respect?"

"Do you respect me?"

"Of course I do."

"Even in spite of what you've had to put up with?"

"Even in spite of that. I know what you can do and be if you put your mind to it. All along I've been telling you that."

"I know. It's just that sometimes I don't believe it myself."

"Then that's another thing you'll have to work out with Dr. Branowitz."

"Dr. Branowitz, Dr. Branowitz . . . it always comes down to him, doesn't it?"

"I have faith in him."

"More than you do in me."

With a sad sigh, Liz put her arm around her brother's waist and gave him a tight squeeze. "*I* have faith in you, but it looks like it's the good doctor who's going to have to help you build that faith in yourself."

4

ALL TOLD, it was a trying afternoon and evening. When Jamie finally agreed to return to San Francisco, he announced that he didn't have money for the ticket. His bank balance was next to nothing, he claimed, and Liz didn't dare ask him where his salary went. So she left him to watch the stew while she dashed to the bank before it closed. By the time she returned, he was having second thoughts again, so she launched into argument once more.

It was nearly nine-thirty before she was finally back home after taking Jamie to the airport and seeing him off. Her headache had escalated to migraine proportions, with the accompanying nausea and sensitivity to light that she'd come to recognize. Her only desire was for her dark room and bed, and utter silence.

When the phone rang shortly after ten, she moaned. Half expecting to hear Jamie on the other end of the line with a song and dance about the plane being delayed, his disembarking and wandering around the terminal, then missing the takeoff, she steeled herself.

It was Donovan.

"Donovan?" She breathed a sigh of sheer relief. "But . . . I thought . . ."

"I just wanted to say hi."

"Where . . . where are you?" She was having trouble getting her own bearings, and couldn't seem to lift her head from the pillow.

"In New Orleans. Uh-oh. I woke you up. Hey, I'm sorry. I didn't dream you'd be in bed at nine."

She put her hand to her head. "I think it's ten here."

There was a pause, then a soft curse. "Hell. I blew it. I was in such a rush to call that I didn't stop to think. Man, I haven't done that in ages and it was only this morning when I turned my watch back." He paused again, but heard no response. "Liz, are you all right?"

The genuine worry in his voice prevented her from lying. "I'm not feeling well, that's all."

"What's wrong?"

"I have an awful headache."

"Did you take something for it?"

"Aspirin. There's not much else I can do."

"Maybe you should call a doctor."

"For a headache? Don't be silly."

"Do you have a temperature?"

"I don't think so."

"Maybe you should find out."

"I don't have a thermometer . . . and besides, it can't be much if it's up, and the aspirin will take care of it, too . . . if I could only get some sleep."

"I can take a hint."

"No, no, Donovan," she returned quickly, and in earnest. "I didn't mean it that way." And she didn't. The sound of Donovan's voice was strangely reassuring, particularly after the to-do with Jamie. "It's just that I didn't sleep well last night, and I lie here with my eyes closed and feel so tired but I *still* can't sleep."

"Try a little warm milk."

She groaned. "I don't think I could get it down."

"How about a warm bath?"

"I *know* I couldn't drink that."

Only when Donovan chuckled did Liz realize what she'd said. In the darkness she smiled. She didn't understand why talking with him should make her feel better, but it did.

"That's better," he said, as though he'd seen her smile. "I'm going to hang up now so you can rest. Can I take you to dinner tomorrow night?"

"That's a sly move."

"What is?"

"Trying to take advantage of me when my brain is all muzzied, but it won't work."

"You won't have dinner with me?"

"No. I'm going to a baby shower for a friend."

"How about Saturday night?"

"I can't."

"Tell me you're tending bar at your cousin's dinner party."

"I don't have a cousin and I can't mix drinks."

"Then you've got a date?"

"Mmm. With this bed. I'm planning to sleep off every bit of the aggravation you've caused me this week." Her annoyance was very much put on. She knew it because at the moment she couldn't seem to remember much of the aggravation he'd caused. He knew it because there was an unmistakable note of humor in her voice.

"Come on, Liz. We could have an early dinner and *then* you could sleep."

"No. Thanks, Donovan, but no."

"Is that firm?"

"Yes."

"No dinner?"

"No."

His exaggerated sigh traveled easily across the miles. "Shot down again. You're terrible for my ego."

"Sorry about that."

"No, you're not. If you were really sorry, you'd reconsider."

"I feel so lousy, Donovan. Please, not now?"

"Okay. Listen, love, you take care. If you don't feel right in the morning, stay home."

"Yes, Donovan."

"And call a doctor."

"Yes, Donovan."

"And when I get back I'll come over and play nurse."

"No, Donovan."

"Good night, love."

"'Night, Donovan." *And thank you for calling.*

BY MORNING her migraine was nothing but a dull ache that responded, at last, to aspirin. She went into the office, determined to bury her worries in work, and she did just that. In addition to making up for all she hadn't done the day before, she met Ray Obermeyer for lunch and put in a most delicately framed plea, then returned and made significant progress on the quarterly report she'd been struggling over.

When one of her fellow workers, newly married and having differences with her husband, rushed into her office in tears, she spent a while calming her. When another dashed in, in a frenzy because the bakery had misplaced the order for the baby-shower cake, Liz calmly called the baker, then another that was willing to create something on such short notice.

Somewhere along the way, she decided against giving up on Donovan Grant.

She wasn't sure when it happened and didn't care to analyze the why of it lest she change her mind. But she drew up preliminary drafts of letters to go to various organizations and individuals associated with the DIG Group, and when Karen came in to see her late that afternoon, Donovan's name didn't come up.

"If there's anything I can do to help with Jamie, just yell," Karen offered, after Liz had briefly explained the immediate problem.

"I will, and thanks, but I think things are going to be okay. I got a call from his lawyer a little while ago—" Jamie himself hadn't bothered to call, but the lawyer evidently knew who was buttering his bread "—and he thinks he can get the girl to drop her complaint. At worst, if she refuses and the case goes forward, Jamie will get a suspended sentence. But he's already back at work, and that's what's important."

"Right. But remember, the offer's open. I've got resources in the Bay Area that I wouldn't hesitate to tap if it would help."

Liz smiled gratefully. "Thanks, Karen. I'll remember."

THE BABY SHOWER, last-minute cake and all, was a grand success. Liz didn't get home until late, so she slept late on Saturday morning, awakening only in time to do a cursory cleaning of the apartment, then shower and dress and meet several friends for the matinee they'd had tickets for for weeks. The show was as good as they'd hoped it would be, as was the dinner they shared afterward. By the time Liz was back in her apartment, she felt relaxed enough to read long into the night. Hence, when her front buzzer rang early Sunday morning, she had to practically pry her eyes open and drag herself from bed.

The sight she met in her peephole brought her fully awake. So much for security precautions, with neighbors who defied them by holding the front door open for strangers. "Go away, Donovan! I'm sleeping!"

His voice was muffled through the door, though distinct nonetheless. "You had all last night to sleep. And I've got breakfast. Come on, open up. The damn coffee's spilled all over the bag and it's burning my hands!"

She pressed her forehead to the door, knowing that if she ignored him long enough he'd leave. But she couldn't ignore him. She'd *never* been able to ignore him. Straightening, she slowly released the chain, slid back the bolt and opened the door.

Without so much as a hello, Donovan dashed past her and headed for the kitchen, which wasn't hard to find since Liz's apartment consisted of a living room, a single bedroom and bath, both of which were off a short hall, and the kitchen, which lay just beyond an archway at the far end of the living room.

"God, what a mess," she heard him say as she slowly approached. Having set the bag on the counter, he was flinging the moisture from his hands into the sink. Then he began to search for a cloth.

"In the cabinet under the sink," she prompted quietly.

He opened it, tore off a lengthy strip of paper towel, mopped his hands, then wadded the towels beneath the sodden bag and went to work unloading what he'd brought.

"Bagels and cream cheese and lox," he announced, placing each package on the counter. "And orange juice." He set the half-pint cartons beside the rest. "And coffee that didn't quite make it."

"I could have made coffee. It's easy enough."

"I know," he said, only then turning to face her. "But I wasn't sure—" his gaze fell and his voice slowed "—if I'd . . . be, uh, welcome . . ."

Only then realizing—and with instant dismay—that she wore nothing but her nightgown, Liz turned and fled to the bedroom, returning only after she'd belted a long terry robe around her and put on slippers.

Donovan had already taken plates from the cupboard and was in the process of setting things on the table. "You looked fine the other way."

"It was my nightgown, for God's sake."

"I know, I know," he muttered beneath his breath, then raised his voice. "But it covered everything. You needn't have worried. Here, have a seat. Uh, on second thought, you'd better not." He gave her a sheepish grin. "I couldn't figure out how to work your coffee maker."

She gave him a well-what-did-you-expect-since-believe-it-or-not-this-isn't-your-home-after-all look, then went by without a word and set up the coffee. She turned to find that he'd already poured her juice into a glass and spread cream cheese on a bagel half, then topped it with lox.

"What would you have done if I didn't like lox?"

"You said you were adventurous when it came to food." He patted the chair next to him. "Have a seat like a good girl. I can't eat until my hostess begins."

"Seems to me you're very much the host." She put one hand on the back of her chair and the other on her hip. "What are you doing here, Donovan?"

"Having breakfast with you—at least I will be once you sit down."

"I told you I didn't want to go out with you."

He held up a hand. "Unnh. We're not 'out.' And you said no to dinner. You didn't say anything against breakfast."

"I thought it was understood," she said, but she sat in the chair anyway and watched Donovan take a mammoth bite of his bagel.

"Mmm." He closed his eyes for the time it took him to chew his mouthful slowly, then swallow. "This . . . is . . . good. There's something about the way the foods blend—bagel and cream cheese and lox—that does it. No one of them is as good by itself, and when you've got all three, that's paradise."

"Donovan, you're changing the subject. I wanted the weekend to myself. I need *some* break from work."

"This isn't work. This is fun."

"But I told you I didn't want that."

"I thought we were friends."

"We are, but—"

"I'm a friend taking care of you at the moment, and I'm telling you to eat."

"I don't need taking care of."

For the first time in the repartee, his confidence faltered and his expression grew serious. "You sounded pretty lousy the other night. Are you feeling better now?"

She stared at him for a final moment, wishing she could fight him but unable to when he grew concerned and gentle, as he was now. "Yes," she answered more softly, "I'm feeling better."

"I'm glad. Eat up. I want to hear what you've been doing since I've been gone."

She bit into the bagel, aware that he was eagerly awaiting her verdict. "You're right," she said at last. "This *is* good."

He smiled and sat back to take a long drink of juice.

"Did everything go well in New Orleans?" she asked.

"Very well. There's a company down there looking for a buyer, a so-called white knight."

"The company's facing a hostile takeover?"

"So you *are* familiar with business antics."

"I have to be in my line of work. Are you looking to buy?"

"Possibly. Not that the company's sure if there *is* a hostile takeover in the offing, but company stocks are being bought by some questionable groups and the directors want to be covered. The company is a major book distributor in the south. It'd be something new for us."

"Is it a sound investment?"

"That's what I've got to find out . . . and fast. The management setup isn't bad, from what I saw in New Orleans. And the scope of the business is huge. But my accountants have to go over the books before we really know much else."

"If the merger went through, it'd be another division of the DIG Group?"

"Right. A diversifying one. I think it could be a good move."

Liz bit into her bagel but her teeth failed to break through the lox, which slithered across the cream cheese and threatened to trail down her chin. In response to her muffled cry, Donovan reached over and secured the stubborn piece so that she could more easily bite it. When she'd finally swallowed what was in her mouth, she was blushing. "Thanks. That was tricky."

He licked the cream cheese on his finger and grinned. "My pleasure. But it's your turn. Tell me about your baby shower."

"There's nothing tricky about a baby shower. On the other hand, I take that back." Smiling, she told him about the cake that nearly wasn't. "In the end it was a great shower, though. Jill—the one who's having the baby—looked fantastic. She worked as Karen's secretary up until two months ago. She's due in another few weeks."

"I bet you'd like to have a baby."

"What makes you say that?"

"The way you lit up when you talked of Jill."

"I'm happy for her. That doesn't mean I want to be in her shoes." At his chiding look, she backed down. "Well, maybe a little. But she didn't have a major investment in a career, so it was an easier decision to make."

"But you admit that you'd like to have a baby—okay, that some teeny-weeny part of you would like it?"

Liz left the table to pour their coffee. She spoke softly, with her back to Donovan. Not for the first time was she stunned by the direction in which he forced her thoughts. Forever and ever, it seemed, she'd managed to avoid thinking of things like a home and family. But he brought it all back, and she grew defensive. "Of course I would. But I doubt it'll happen."

"Why not?"

"Because . . . I'm busy with other things."

"That's a matter of choice, isn't it? If you wanted to be less busy, you could."

"But I choose not to be. I like my work. I like my life as it is. Milk, no sugar?"

"You remembered."

"How could I forget? You made quite a thing over my adding two sugars to mine that day at lunch."

"I was only kidding."

She turned then and smiled as she set his coffee before him. "I know. I'm learning."

"I'm glad," he said with such quiet intensity that for a minute Liz couldn't think of a thing to say. Concentrating on her own coffee cup, she sat down dumbly. "What else have you done," Donovan went on quietly, "besides go to a baby shower?"

"I worked. I drew up some preliminary letters for you to see. Unfortunately they're at the office. I didn't expect to . . . see you sooner."

"That's okay. You were right. The weekend isn't for working. It'll be soon enough for me to see them tomorrow."

"I think we should get something out this week. Each day that passes is a day lost. I also made a few calls to some press contacts, and I've got a list of others to phone this week. As soon as the letters are out, we ought to start in with the newspapers and electronic media."

"Sounds good."

She studied him for a minute. "You're very laid-back about it all."

"Shouldn't I be?"

"Well, it *is* a crisis situation. One of your divisions— your very first—is in danger of dying a slow and costly death. I'd have thought you'd be champing at the bit to get a campaign rolling to prevent it."

He shrugged. "There's no point in doing it if it's not done right and to do it right takes sane planning. Besides," he said grinning brightly, "I've hired *you* to do the champing. I know you'll save my baby."

She smirked. "You do, do you."

"Yup. So, what else have you been up to since I went away?"

"What *else*? There are only so many hours in a day, and you were only gone for one day."

"But I didn't see you for two others. You couldn't have been working or giving baby showers all that time."

"You're right. I cleaned house. And saw some friends yesterday afternoon."

"And you slept."

"Yes."

"What brought on the headache the other night? I hope it wasn't me."

If only he hadn't sounded so truly concerned she might have had a chance. But he had, and she didn't, so quite helplessly she found herself talking of Jamie. Donovan listened, asking thoughtful questions from time to time, expressing sympathy, giving support. As she'd done with Karen, so Liz told only of the most recent crisis. She wasn't *that* taken with the man's interest that she'd go into a family history. Unfortunately, that was just what Donovan wanted.

"You haven't talked of your family at all. This is the first time you've mentioned a word. Are your parents still alive?"

She hesitated for an instant, tracing the curved handle of her coffee mug. "My father, yes. My mother died years ago."

"Is he still in Baltimore?" When she looked up sharply, he explained. "You mentioned the first time we met that you were from Baltimore."

"I forgot. Yes, he's still in Baltimore."

"What does he do?"

"Sells insurance."

"Baltimore's not that far. It must be nice to be able to see him often."

"I don't. We're not very close."

"How come?"

"Oh," she waffled, and scrunched up her nose, "you know how it can be. We have different ideas about lots of things."

"You're right; I do know how that can be. But still, often the differences fade as we get older."

"They haven't," she responded quietly.

"How about Jamie? Barring emergencies like the one this week, do you see him much?"

"He's far away. It's pretty expensive . . . flying across the country."

"You can afford it."

"Well," she sighed, unable to refute his claim, "it's still hard. I do call him once a week."

"But you three must get together for holidays."

"Actually, no."

"Then what *do* you do . . . for Thanksgiving and Christmas and all?"

She looked up then and forced a smile. "I'm usually with friends. Why does this feel like an inquisition?"

"I'm just curious. It's strange." He did look puzzled, and that took the edge off his comments. "I'd have pictured you surrounded by family as well as friends. You're so giving and easy to talk to."

"Coming from you that's a compliment, since you've certainly seen my acid side."

"Nah. Never acid. Maybe nervous or defensive. But you're getting over it. You're more comfortable with me now than you were. I can tell."

"Oh?"

"Sure. Just look at you. You're fresh from bed, sitting here in your nightgown and robe having Sunday-morning breakfast with me."

"I'm only doing this so you'll see reason," she retorted defiantly. "I'm perfectly ugly in the morning. My hair's a mess and my skin is as sallow—"

"Are you kidding? Whoever told you that?"

"I've got eyes. I see me this way every morning."

Donovan's voice grew very quiet. "You're not looking through *my* eyes, and I see something very different."

"Donovan, don't—"

"I see a warm and gentle woman, who looks that much softer and more desirable coming straight from bed."

Liz jumped from her chair, but he caught her wrist and, tipping her off balance, brought her down on his lap.

"You don't believe me, do you?" he asked.

"Not for a minute. Now let me up." She was holding her body rigid, but Donovan seemed unperturbed.

"Not until I show you how you affect me first thing in the morning."

She tried to rise, but his arm tightened about her waist. When he put his lips to her neck, she began to squirm.

"Hold still," he commanded, his breath warm against her skin. "You smell so good."

"It's . . . it's the fabric softener—" she pushed against his arms, but to no avail "—that I put in . . . the wash . . . Donovan, let go!"

He didn't bother to answer, but began to lightly kiss the underside of her jaw. She closed her eyes and tried to rein in her senses, but the war she was waging was hopeless because she could smell the clean, lemon-tinged scent of his hair, could feel the liquid heat of his mouth, could fully appreciate the strength of the body that imprisoned her so effortlessly. He was male from head to toe, and, God help her, he made her feel female.

A final moan of protest slipped from her throat and then he was kissing her, warming her from the inside out, showing her the unbelievable pleasure to be gotten from the meeting and meshing of lips and teeth and tongues. Before she knew it she was clutching his shoulders, bunching the wool of his sweater in her fists as though she were drowning and needed a lifeline.

He kissed her again and again, taking but the briefest of breaths between forays. She couldn't pull away because he suddenly seemed her sustenance, more so even than air or light or the blood that pumped so rapidly through her veins.

Her lips were against his hair then, and she was cupping his head while his mouth moved lower, lower. His hands, which had been stroking her from shoulder to hip, moved frontward, gently raising her breasts without quite touching them, until his face was buried between their gentle swells.

Sustenance or sustainer... for a minute she wondered whether she was the receiver or the giver. Donovan seemed to be feeding off her nearness, as though she offered him something he couldn't live without. She knew it wasn't so, but for the moment she was willing to believe that she was different and special and, yes, desirable. He muddled her mind, but she loved it. It was fantasy-playing at its most glorious.

His fingers skimmed her breasts en route to the tiny buttons at her throat, then he was releasing them one by one, covering each inch of revealed flesh with his mouth. He'd just about reached her breasts when she realized what was happening.

"No..." she whispered, but he was spreading the vee of her robe farther apart to reach those buttons it had hidden. "Don't...oh, no..." Torn apart inside, she begged, "No...please, no..." She was whimpering and close to tears as utter terror filled her. It was only the latter that gave her the strength to dig her fingers into his neck and tug him away. When he looked up in surprise, she clutched the lapels of the robe close together.

"I...I don't understand," he began hoarsely.

"You can't do that," she whispered with her head tucked low.

He took a ragged breath. "But...you were...it felt..."

She was shaking her head, trying to free herself of the thoughts that tormented her, but she couldn't.

"Elizabeth?"

In response she moved awkwardly to her own chair. Fleeing the room would have been too much to ask of her trembling legs, so she simply sat with her knuckles white at the neck of her robe, her head bent.

Donovan raised a hand and stroked her hair once, lightly, then sat back in his chair and closed his eyes for a minute. When he'd opened them, he was in control.

"Why don't you get dressed," he suggested quietly, gently. "We can take a ride up to my place and go for a walk in the woods."

Liz didn't answer for a while, and when she did it was still without raising her eyes. "I don't think...I should."

"Why not? That was the main thing I had in mind when I came over here so early."

His place. She finally looked up, but timidly. "That's right. It's your hideaway. Why aren't you there now?"

"Because I'm here."

She frowned. "How *did* you get here?"

He gave her a gentle smile. "I drove."

"No, I mean, how did you know where I live?"

"The same way I was able to call you the other night. The phone book. 'E. Jerome.' The initial is a sure sign of a woman, and since there were no other E. Jeromes, only Edwards and Edgars and Eugenes and Evans—"

"Where does Innis come from?"

"Innis?"

"Your middle name. I thought it was so clever to call your group the DIG Group, since you started out growing foods and all, until I realized that those were your initials. I read the Innis part on your biographical sketch."

"It's my mother's maiden name. She hated to see it die, particularly since her only brother has four daughters."

Liz nodded, then, uncomfortable, looked away again.

"How about it?" he asked softly. "I've got to come back to the city tonight, anyway. We could take a ride up and just relax. It's a beautiful day. There might not be too many more like it."

"I know. But I . . . I'm not sure . . ."

"I wouldn't try anything Liz. I swear it. I just want to spend some time with you. Totally innocent. Brother and sister, if you'd like." Inwardly he cringed at his own offer, but he knew he'd settle for that if it was all she could give him at the moment. She charmed him with her innocence, her lack of demand. He simply needed to be with her.

It wasn't so much what he'd said as the undercurrent of urgency in his voice that swayed Liz. She remembered when he'd been kissing her, when she'd felt, albeit dreamily, that he needed her desperately. The urgency she'd sensed then was similar in its way to that she heard now. And she couldn't resist. Perhaps it was what she needed in life—to be needed. She thrived on having friends come to her with problems, thrived on doing favors for other people. And Donovan was her... friend, wasn't he?

"Brother and sister?" she echoed, eyeing him shyly.

"Brother and sister. I promise."

She stood slowly, dropping her hands to fidget nervously with her belt. "I really shouldn't be doing this."

Donovan stood, physically turned her and gave her a light shove. "Get dressed. I'll clean this stuff up. If we don't leave soon we'll miss the best part of the day."

THEY ARRIVED AT THE HOUSE shortly before noon. As Donovan had said, it was a beautiful day, all the more beautiful with the woodlands at their autumnal best.

"You miss this in the city," Liz mused, standing by the side of the car and taking the scenery in. "I think the color's at its height. It's lovely."

Her smile of delight was what Donovan found most lovely, but he didn't say it. Though he didn't understand why, she didn't take to his compliments. And he had promised...

"Why don't you wander out back. I'll open up the house and then we'll go exploring."

She nodded and headed around the house, walking on a mat of pine needles, occasionally overstepping gnarled fingers of tree roots that had found their way to the earth's surface. The sound of gurgling water lured her on, and she soon found herself by a brook that wound through Donovan's property and into the woods. It was charming and peaceful. She felt decidedly cheerful.

Kneeling, she ran a finger through the clear water, then tipped her head back and basked in the sun's warmth.

It was in that position that Donovan found her moments later. "Nice?"

"Mmm. Wonderful. Such a marvelous retreat."

"The brook doesn't freeze till dead of winter, and then it's beautiful in a different way." He sank to the ground on a cushion of moss several feet from her. "Early some mornings you can see deer here."

"I thought I saw a chipmunk as I was walking back."

"You probably did. They're all over the place. And rabbits, and woodchucks, even a fox once in a while."

"A fox?"

"Oh, the fox is harmless enough. He runs in the opposite direction well before you do." He was trying not to smile. "No, it's the skunks you have to worry about. Lazy buggers, skunks are. You walk out in your own backyard to admire the moon, and a pudgy black-and-white thing waddles across your path. You don't know whether to freeze or run, and the damned animal continues to saunter, just as cocky as you please, while you're racking your brain trying to remember what it is that will get out the stench if you're sprayed."

"Have you ever been?" she asked, wide-eyed.

"Once."

"What *does* get the smell out?"

"A quick trip to the nearest dump with your clothes . . . or a bonfire in the backyard. And cologne, gobs of it, for days."

She laughed at his drawling tone and readily let him draw her to her feet and toward a path that led into the woods. The growth on either side was lush and had the poignant fragrance of autumn. The crackle of twigs underfoot blended with the sounds of the breeze and the scurry of wildlife that eluded Liz's untrained eye. Donovan's eye wasn't as untrained. In a voice as soft and airy as a whisper of the leaves overhead, he pointed out various animal habitats and identified the calls of the migrating birds.

In time they came to an open meadow whose swaying grasses were gilded by the sun. Shrugging out of their sweaters in deference to the warmth of the early-afternoon air, they walked to an old tree stump and sat, side by side, enjoying the serenity in silence. At length Donovan broke it with an indrawn breath, as though he'd been millions of miles away and had suddenly returned.

"When I was a kid, my parents used to take us off to fancy resorts in the mountains. At first I thought it was boring; I wanted to be *doing* things. By the time I was fifteen I was arguing that it was a grand waste of money to pay so much for a luxury resort, when we could just walk into the nearest park if we wanted fresh air." He chuckled. "I think I was missing the point."

"Which was?"

"To get us all together. To break the routine of our everyday lives. To remind us that we were a family and that, even in the woods, miles from civilization, we had each other. I wish I'd understood it sooner."

"Maybe you did."

"What do you mean?"

"Maybe that's what you were rebelling against, the idea that you were dependent on others. You were trying to form an identity of your own, and the reminder that you were irrevocably part of a larger group, in this case your family, was hard for you to accept."

"Well, I wish I had accepted it. I missed out on a lot of warmth because I was too stubborn to try to see things as my parents did."

"Most kids are that way."

"Were you?"

"I suppose. Then again, my situation was different."

"How so?"

"With my mother dead and all, we didn't have much of a family life."

"Didn't your dad do things with you?"

"Not often. He was busy with work, doubly busy, he said, since he couldn't travel because of us."

"How old were you?"

"When my mother died? I was ten. Jamie was six."

Donovan winced. "It must have been tough for *all* of you."

"It was. But she'd been sick for a long time. Her death was a blessing."

"Awful to think of death as a blessing." He looked off into the distance. "It's what frightens me most sometimes, because there's still so much I haven't done."

"But you're so successful."

"Professionally, yes. Personally, well, that's up for grabs." He seemed about to say more, then changed his mind. "How did your father manage after your mother died?"

"Not well."

"What do you mean?"

"He'd always been something of a cynic. Her death made things worse."

"Who took care of Jamie and you?"

"Oh, we had a housekeeper. We'd always had help because my mother wasn't able to do much, but in the later years of her illness Dad got harder to live with, so there was a pretty fair turnover."

"Not great when two kids need stability and love."

She lowered her voice and looked down. "No."

"Did you *ever* do things as a family? You mentioned once that you traveled."

"Oh, yes. My father had certain priorities, one of which was traveling. Actually, it was a matter of taking us with him on business trips when they coincided with school vacations."

"Not much fun, then?"

"Not much. Well, maybe I shouldn't say that. We did our share of sightseeing."

Donovan's voice was tight. "With a paid guide, while your father worked?"

She looked at him in surprise, then quickly recovered. "It wasn't bad. Actually, some of the guides were more fun than Dad would have been. They were certainly knowledgeable."

"But they weren't your father. That must have hurt."

"Lots of things hurt. You just learn to concentrate on those things that don't."

They'd come full circle. "And that's where you differ from your father."

"It's . . . one of the ways. He also happens to be a chauvinist. He can't understand the work I do, other than to feel that I'm taking a job away from a man who needs it to support his family."

Donovan was grinning. "What do you say to that?"

"Not a thing. I can't change the way he thinks. It'd be a waste of my time and effort to try, and there are too many things I'd rather be doing."

"Does *he* seek out any contact with you?"

"No."

"He must be a lonely man."

"I wouldn't know," Liz stated simply.

Donovan couldn't help but think it was odd that she was so open and willing to discuss others' feelings and motivations, yet totally turned off to her own father.

"Is there other family—aunts and uncles and cousins?"

"Nothing on Dad's side—well, he did have a sister but he never saw her. There were some relatives on my mother's side, but we lost contact with them soon after she died." She shot him a sad glance. "Loving family I've got, isn't it?"

But he was feeling a sadness of his own. "I could have had all you didn't, and I threw it away. It's pathetic, when you stop to think of it."

"Not pathetic. And you didn't throw it away. You simply . . . deferred it."

"Yeah. But I lost a whole lot in the process."

"You'll gain it back, and it'll be that much more meaningful for the value you put on it now."

"Some things you can't gain back. My mother's gone. My father's getting older. My sister and brother have their own families and lives. And David . . . well, those early years are gone."

Liz put her hand on Donovan's arm and shook it gently. "Where's that old optimism, Donovan? It's not like you to bemoan the fates."

"I know," he said, his eyes meeting hers. "But you bring some things out, make me think about others. You're good to talk to. You listen and respond. I know I've said as much before, but I mean it. You seem to be everyone's confidante. Who's yours?"

She laughed, but there was a melancholy sound to it. "I'm the lady of steel. I don't need a confidante. And anyway, I think I've told you more today..." Her voice trailed off and she looked away, realizing how much she *had* said, perplexed that she should have told Donovan so much about herself. It was frightening to think of how easy it had been, to envision becoming dependent on his ear, only to have it withdrawn.

"You're cold. You've got goose bumps." He reached for her sweater. "Better put this on."

She did, and frightened of pushing her, Donovan began to talk of other things. They left their tree stump and walked farther before finally retracing their route to the house. By the time he'd built a fire—she argued that it was too early in the season, but he insisted that a fire in the hearth was good for the soul—she felt relaxed and surprisingly happy.

True to his word, Donovan was perfectly brotherly, though so much more thoughtful than Jamie had ever been that Liz had to redefine the term. Jamie leaned on her. Jamie took from her. Jamie used her. And she let him. It was the least she could do to make up for all she hadn't been able to do when they'd been younger.

She and Donovan made dinner together and ate before the fire, talking all the while of inconsequential things that somehow seemed less inconsequential what with the insights the other lent them. Liz was stunned that she and Donovan shared so many views. And while they also had their differences, they were able to discuss and accept them.

All too soon, the day ended. While Donovan drove back to the city, Liz sat contented in the passenger's seat, dozing at the last. She was groggy when he walked her to her apartment, and she only half heard herself ask him in for coffee before she dozed off again on the sofa.

When she awoke the brother was gone, replaced by the man who'd been tethered all day.

5

LIZ OPENED HER EYES to find herself cradled in Donovan's arms. His head was buried against her neck, where his lips moved lightly, moistly. She sighed softly and indulged herself the momentary luxury, pretending she was dreaming and that this was her dashing knight, the man set upon the earth for no other reason than to protect her, to care for her, to give her what she'd never dared wish for.

Her lashes lowered as she dreamed, and her fingers combed through the hair at his nape. It was thick and soft and yielded vibrantly, beckoning her touch.

She felt Donovan shift slightly and tipped her head to ease his access, only to have her chin brought back by his gentle hand when his lips sought hers. What had been totally new once was now familiar and irresistible. She responded to the lead of his mouth, opening her own and welcoming him with a verve that was instinctive. She didn't have to clutch his shoulders this time because the drowning sensation she'd known that morning seemed now more exciting than overwhelming. Instead her hands found their way to his back, moving slowly, charting by inches the sturdy cording of muscles they found.

A tiny part of her tried to temper the fantasy, but failed. With each tilt of his lips, with each sweep of his tongue she was more deeply enveloped in it and in the glorious sense of awakening that it spawned. Her body thrummed with pleasure. Warm bursts of delight spread through her.

Drugged by his sensual assault, she made no protest when he shifted her to lie on the cushions, freeing his hands to span her waist, then her ribs. But she wanted more; her breasts swelled in anticipation. A small purr of satisfaction slipped from her throat when he gently covered them and began to move his palms in devastatingly light circles over their fullness.

Even had his mouth not continued to monopolize hers, she couldn't have uttered a word, for she was momentarily beyond rational thought, totally swept away in a world of sensation. She arched her back, strained closer to those heavenly hands, and was rewarded when he increased the pressure.

She was gasping when he released her lips and slid his mouth across her cheek to her ear, but she could hear his own ragged breathing and it perfectly justified her state. She became so wrapped up with what he was doing to her ear that she didn't notice he'd slipped his hand under her shirt and sweater until she felt an encompassing warmth on her breasts, distinctly different from the simple nylon of her bra. Her flesh felt seared, yet it ached for more, and her body conveyed the message quite eloquently.

The tiny part of her that had tried to break through did so again, but she fought its warning. For so many long years she hadn't known what she'd been missing, but she knew it now, and it felt right. The quivering tendrils that shot to the pit of her stomach when his fingers homed in on her budded nipples had her arching her hips. Everything in her body responded so naturally to Donovan that surely it was meant to be, she reasoned from amid her dream.

Then he was kissing her again, sliding his body over hers, abandoning her breasts to shape her hip, the inside of her thigh, the warm apex that had never been so shaped, so caressed. Donovan's deep groan sparked another warning in the back of her mind, but she had to know what came next, where the anticipation that coiled in her belly would lead.

Somehow he was between her thighs then, rubbing against her, undulating his hips in a way that taunted rather than eased. But when he raised his body to allow his fingers a hasty release of the snap of her jeans, the sound reverberated in her brain and her bubble popped.

"Oh, God!" She gulped and grabbed his wrists to halt the work of his hands. "No, Donovan...oh, my God...stop!"

His breath was rough and panting as he held himself over her and stared down incredulously.

Her eyes were wide and pleading. "Please," she whispered, and swallowed convulsively, "please...I can't..."

"Sure, you can," he murmured, lowering his head to kiss her, but she turned her face aside and squeezed her eyes shut. Her body, so hot and pliant moments before, was suddenly rigid. He raised his head and stared at her, dropped his gaze to study the stiff way she lay, then slowly pushed himself up until he sat an arm's length away. "All right, Liz," he said with remarkable

calm, "you're going to tell my why. You're going to tell
me why a woman in this day and age can't make love
with a man who turns her on."

Drawing her knees sideways, Liz rolled up, then
huddled into the opposite corner of the sofa. Her arms
were crossed over her waist, covering the condemning
snap of her jeans. She stared at the floor, wincing when
Donovan spoke with greater force.

"Tell me, Elizabeth. You owe me an explanation. It's
not right to lead a man on. Didn't anyone ever teach
you that?"

Mutely, she shook her head. She didn't see Donovan
thrust an agitated hand through his hair, but she heard
his growl of frustration and felt worse.

"Why did you ask me to stop?"

"Because . . . I don't want to . . . make love."

"Sure as hell could've fooled me, what with the way
you were responding." When she grimaced and tightened her arms around herself, he modulated his tone.
"Okay. We agree that it's not a matter of physical re-
vulsion. And you've said that there isn't another man
in your life. Was there one in the past who hurt you? A
minute ago I saw terror in your eyes. That had to be it.
You've been abused."

She quickly shook her head, unable to speak, much
less look at him. He was too close to the truth, but it
wasn't the way he thought and she just couldn't go into
it.

"*Was* there someone?" Again she shook her head.
"Never?" She shook her head a third time. Donovan
seemed to hold his breath, then let it out slowly. His
voice was quiet. "You're a virgin." When she didn't re-

spond but squeezed her eyes shut, he coaxed her more gently. "Elizabeth? Tell me. Please. I have to know. Is it something about me? Or you? Or the situation?"

"It's me," she whispered at last.

"You are a virgin."

Very slowly, she nodded.

He was closing the distance between them then, taking her in his arms, holding her tenderly. "God, Liz. I wish I'd realized it sooner. It's just that I didn't expect...I mean, you're nearly thirty...I just assumed..." He pressed her head to his chest and stroked her hair until he felt her first sign of relaxation. "Do you know how wonderful that is, what a gift? Do you have any idea how good it makes me feel to know that I'll be the first?"

Any momentary relaxation he'd felt in her vanished, and she levered herself away. "You won't be," she stated sharply. With the dissolution of her passion-induced dream, she saw the light. Donovan's words had helped. She was a virgin, to him little more than a new and rather pathetic challenge. And he was the master game player.

"That doesn't make sense."

"To me it does."

"You're a passionate woman, Liz."

"What does *that* have to do with anything?" Her eyes sparked with anger, and Donovan stared, disbelieving.

"I don't understnd," he finally managed. "We go well together both intellectually and physically—"

"No, we don't. *You* go well with just about anybody. Not me."

"What's that supposed to mean?"

Returning his gaze, she found her anger dissipating. In its stead was a soul-rending sadness. "It means that I'm not good for you. You can have any woman you want. You can take your pick of the most beautiful of the beautiful, the most brilliant of the brilliant. You don't need me. I'm just a . . . a plaything."

"Like hell you are," he growled, but Liz was jumping from the sofa and pacing across the room.

"You can do better, Donovan," she said with her back to him. "You can do much better than me."

"Is that what you think? Man, you're crazy! Do you have any idea how long I've looked for the right woman?"

"And you haven't been able to find her, so you're temporarily amusing yourself with me."

"Damn it, that's *not* what I meant. You're jumping to conclusions, and every one of them is wrong. I'm not 'amusing' myself with you. And there's nothing temporary about what I want."

She gave a bitter laugh. "Which would make hell that much hotter for me."

Donovan was off the sofa then and turning her around. Though his hand was insistent, his gaze was beseechful. "You don't believe that I'm serious, when I say I am. Why is it you find it so hard to believe that I want you?"

She spared him a pained glance before looking away. "I believe that you want me. I'm not that dumb that I don't know when a man's aroused."

"Forget sex. I'm talking in the broader sense."

"I can't forget sex. It . . . tinges everything else."

"It doesn't have to," he countered softly, "not that I
see it as being a problem. We'd be great together, Liz.
I've held you and kissed you. I've felt you respond. You
body is perfect for mine. If you'd let me, I'd show you.
We could go into your bedroom and undress and—"

"No!" she cried in fright, pressing her hands to her
ears so that she wouldn't have to hear more. When she
saw that he'd stopped speaking and was staring at her
in amazement, she lowered her hands and pleaded.
"Look at me, Donovan. I'm nothing. I'm plain and unattractive and—"

"You've hinted at that before, but you're wrong.
There's nothing plain and unattractive about you.
You're a beautiful woman from the inside out."

"Now that," she stated baldly, "is an outright lie."

"I don't lie, Liz. You just refuse to see what I'm saying." He put his hands on her shoulders to hold her
when she looked about to bolt again. "Okay, so you're
not Miss America. I'm not Mr. America, for that matter. But there are things inside you—warmth and sensitivity and generosity—that make you shine."

"My hair is yuk brown. My eyes are sunken. My nose
sits in the middle of my face like a bump on a log. My
lips are bottom-heavy. And my body...God, I wouldn't
know *where* to begin on that."

"I would know, because I've felt it beneath mine. It
curves where it should and pulses when it should and
it turns me on in a way no other body had ever done."
He shook her shoulders lightly. "Beauty isn't skin-deep,
Liz. It comes from within. At least true beauty does.
And that's what I see in you."

Liz sighed and dropped her chin. "I don't need flattering, Donovan. I'm a realist." She paused. "I think you'd better leave now. It's been a nice day, but I'm really exhausted, and I have to be in the office early tomorrow."

"You'd just forget this whole thing as if it never happened?"

She tipped up her chin and held it firm. "I already have."

He eyed her intently for a minute, then dropped his hands from her shoulders and stepped back. "Okay. I've got a little pride left. Have it your way for now. If it's work you want, work you'll get. I'll stop in tomorrow afternoon to look over the letters."

"I have an appointment at one. You'll have to make it after two-thirty."

"I'll see you at three then." One corner of his mouth curved into a wry half smile. "Sweet dreams, Liz."

She simply stared at him until he turned and left. Then she crumpled onto the sofa and cried.

BY THREE O'CLOCK the following afternoon Liz was all business. She had separate letters drawn up, one for stockholders and investors, one for employees, one for distributors, each with its own appropriate slant. Donovan read then carefully, made several minor suggestions, then approved them. He ran through the list of media outlets she'd prepared and asked questions about one or two, but could find no fault with her overall plan.

If he was more somber than usual, Liz told herself to be grateful. She'd let things go too far, and it was her own fault. She should never have agreed to spend Sunday with him...nor let him get so close to her that she'd lost control. She didn't know why she'd done it. She'd never harbored illusions of loving and being loved by a man before, yet Donovan did strange, strange things to her.

On one level she missed the twinkle in his eye, the verbal sparring that had almost always had sexual overtones, his teasing. On another, a more rational level, she knew that this way was better. It was more businesslike. It was more conducive to productivity. It was how things should be with a client, and that was all Donovan Grant could ever be.

THE WEEK PASSED QUICKLY. Liz completed the quarterly report she'd been working on. She made headway with arrangements for publicity for the *Women's Journal*. She spoke with Cheryl Obermeyer and learned that Ray had indeed calmed down and seemed content, for the moment, to stick with his current responsibilities.

The DIG Group letters went out, and Donovan's media blitz took shape. Liz met on five different occasions with various media representatives. She spent time on the phone with others. By the end of the week she was able to present Donovan with a list of a dozen appearances and interviews she'd set up for the next two weeks, with additional ones in different parts of the country still to be confirmed and scheduled.

For his part, Donovan was thoroughly accessible. When she called, he came. When she spoke, he listened. She prepped him on ways to most effectively handle the press, posing questions interviewers might ask, then helping him to analyze and strengthen his answers.

At each of their meetings, and there were three that week, his behavior was without fault. He was the perfect gentleman, the quick-minded and attentive businessman. She couldn't even begrudge him showing up one day in a sweater and jeans, because her hungry eye savored it and she indulged herself the passing fancy. Indeed, his outward manner was justification that she'd been right in what she'd said and done. He'd obviously and, without great effort, given up on her as a playmate. His attraction to her wasn't that strong after all.

Of course she knew nothing about the meeting he had with her boss.

"I need your help, Karen," he said soon after he'd entered her office. It was shortly after his third session with Liz. "Something's odd, and for the life of me, I can't figure it out."

"That's not like you, Donovan. You're not often . . . perplexed."

"I'm dead serious, so you can wipe that grin off your face, friend. I've got a problem, and it's all your fault."

"Mine?"

"You were the one who introduced me to Elizabeth Jerome."

Teasing suddenly forgotten, Karen frowned. "What's wrong? You're not displeased with what she's doing, are you?"

"Of course not. She's wonderful. Insightful, efficient and a hard worker."

"Then . . ."

"It's her. Personally. I can't seem to get through to her."

Now that she knew the problem had nothing to do with work, Karen eased back and smiled. "That's *really* not like you. I never thought you'd have trouble on that score."

"*No* score. And it doesn't make sense. We get along perfectly when it comes to work, and even when it comes to doing simple things for fun. I brought her up to my place last Sunday and we had a terrific time."

"But you can't get her into bed," Karen prompted dryly.

"It's not that that's all I want, but there does seem to be a major stumbling block in that area."

"I don't know, Donovan. You must be losing your touch with age."

"I am *not* losing my touch, and stop laughing at me, Karen. You seem to think this is pretty funny, but I don't."

"It's okay," she cooed, her eyes still dancing, "I'm told it's a common problem. May be part of a midlife crisis—okay, okay, I'll be serious. You are, aren't you?"

"Serious? Very. I'm taken with Liz. But then, you knew I would be. That's why you threw us together."

"I didn't 'throw' you together. I simply assigned her to your case."

"Well, she's on it, and now I'm on hers. How well do you know her, Karen?"

"As well as anybody, I guess, which isn't saying all that much. She's a private person when it comes to her inner thoughts and feelings."

"She says that there haven't been any men in her life."

"Believe it. I've tried before, but nothing's worked."

"Any ideas why not?"

"She claims not to be interested. She says she's perfectly happy with her life as it is now and doesn't need anything else. I could almost believe her. She loves her work and she's got loads of friends. People take to her because—"

"She's such a great listener. I know. She's a born counselor. Her instincts about people's emotions are solid, and she has all the patience in the world when it comes to hand holding." His voice dropped. "But she doesn't have relationships with men."

"Not sexual ones."

"Then she does have male *friends*?"

"I'm not sure about even that. She gets along well with male clients, but whether any of them have become friends or whether she has any other long-standing male friends, I just don't know." Karen looked at him, hesitated, then spoke. "I do know that you threaten her somehow. After she met you the first time, she asked me to take her off the case."

"She really did?"

"Mmm. But she couldn't give me a reason, at least not one I thought to be legitimate. She did a lot of beating around the bush, but I think she was really scared."

"But why. . . and of me, of all people?"

"Come on, Donovan," Karen drawled. "You know the answer to that as well as me. You affect her in ways that no one else ever has."

"That's no cause for her to be terrified, yet she is. I see it in her eyes sometimes. Sheer terror."

"I asked her once . . ." Karen began, only to bite her lip.

"You asked her what?"

"I really shouldn't betray her confidence this way."

"Karen, I'm on my way to falling in *love* with the woman. I'm asking you to help me understand her. Something's got to be hanging her up so she can't let herself go. And I'm not talking only of sex."

Hearing the desperation in his voice, Karen resolved her dilemma in his favor. "I asked her if she'd been raped."

He hadn't had the guts to ask it as bluntly himself. "And?"

"She said no."

"Do you think she was telling the truth? Women often feel guilt after something like that. They come to believe that they somehow invited it."

"No," Karen mused thoughtfully, "I think she was being honest. But I agree with you. Something *is* hanging her up."

"Any theories?"

Karen shrugged with her brows. "I could speculate . . . but I'm not sure it'd be fair to her."

"It'd be only fair to *me*. Go on. Speculate. I'm listening."

"There's got to be something in her background that's deeply affected her. Do you know anything about her brother?"

"Jamie? She told me about him last week."

"He's been a worry to her for years. She feels responsible for him. He's constantly getting into trouble, and I have to ask myself why. When you see a kid like that who can't seem to settle down, there's usually a reason."

Donovan pondered that for a minute. "I know she didn't have a happy home life when she was growing up. Her father sounds like a bastard."

"You know more than I do then. She's never said much of anything about the man to me, other than a passing reference here or there."

"She didn't say all that much to me, either, and it wasn't that she was blatantly critical. She seemed almost...detached when she spoke of him, like he's part of her past that she can factually accept but that she'd just as soon never tangle with again. I can't believe she's sexually hung up on him. Maybe angry deep down inside at the way he let Jamie and her down. But sexually hung up? Nah."

"Did she say anything about her parents' personal relationship?"

"No. Her mother died early on and was sick for a long time before that. I doubt there was much of a sexual thing there, if you're thinking that maybe Liz was traumatized by something she'd seen. As for Jamie's problems, they could well have been from lack of interest on the father's part."

Karen made a face. "We sound like a pair of amateur psychiatrists. I don't know, Donovan. I just don't know. But listen," she leaned forward, "don't give up on Liz. I think she's a fantastic girl."

"You don't have to tell *me* that. And believe me, I have no *intention* of giving up on her, not while there's still a chance."

"I believe you," she said with a smile. "That's the Donovan I *do* know."

THE FOLLOWING WEEK the media campaign Liz had engineered for Donovan began. She was present during most of the interviews, some of which were held at his office, others at restaurants over breakfast or lunch, still others at television or radio studios.

The week after that they made day trips to hit the media in Boston, Philadelphia and Washington, and by the end of that second week, Liz was confident that the campaign would be a success. Wherever he went, Donovan was received well. He was personable, articulate and effective. He handled even sticky questions with ease and managed to charm the most wary of interviewers. Though it would be a while longer before they knew whether the public was buying their case, Liz was personally pleased with the articles that appeared in print. She studied videotapes over and over again with the same satisfaction that was expressed by other members of her firm and Donovan's.

During the two-week period Liz found herself enjoying Donovan again. He made no mention of what had happened the night at her apartment. Nor did he try anything further, other than to issue an occasional invitation to dinner that she refused in the same teasing tone in which it was offered. But she always felt an inkling of excitement waking up on a morning when she knew she'd be seeing him, and he never failed to make her laugh at least once on those days. If there was method to his madness in giving her space, she was unaware of it. She only knew that she enjoyed talking business with him—which they did regularly—and that on practically any other subject he was good for conversation.

Then it came time for him to travel, to meet the press in Chicago and Detroit and Dallas and the West. When he launched his own campaign to entice her along, she politely but firmly refused, insisting that he'd been fully trained, that he handled himself like a pro, that she simply couldn't be spared that long from the office. In fact, she was fearful of what might happen given a hotel room in a distant place. She wanted no opportunity for mischief. She didn't think she could cope with that. It was going to be difficult enough for her when her job was done and she no longer saw him from day to day. A small part of her had grown dependent on his friendship, and she wasn't sure how, without the convenience of working together, they'd be able to maintain it.

As it happened, while he was on the road he called her at least once a day in the office and then again at her apartment at night. He seemed to need to know she was there, to discuss his day with her, to hear about what she'd done herself. And again they lapsed into the sexual bantering she'd thought they'd left behind. She told herself that it was the distance between them that inspired it, told herself that Donovan needed this warm touch, told herself that it was really harmless. But she spent more and more time thinking about it, thinking about *him*, thinking about what she felt and what she believed, and fearing that, eventually, there would be trouble.

It began the following week, on the very day that Donovan returned from Seattle, the last stop on his tour. She'd just arrived in the office when her phone rang.

"I'm back!"

Her heart flip-flopped and she broke into a smile. "So you are. How did it go?"

"Not bad. Would have been better if you'd been along."

"Flattery will get you nowhere. Did you make it to all the interviews?" There had been some question, even as late as the morning before, as to whether several of those scheduled would pan out.

"All except the one at the cable station. But the others went well. And I'm glad to be back. Listen, I'm going home to get some sleep. How about dinner tonight?"

"I can't, Donovan. I'm meeting with another client."

"Oh. How about breakfast tomorrow then?"

"Why don't you just come by here in the morning? I have a nine-o'clock appointment, but I should be free by ten."

"We could have breakfast at eight. Come on, Liz. I want to see you."

"Ten o'clock?"

There was a long pause before he answered. "Right. See you then."

But the following morning he called her at seven to say that he had to make an emergency trip to New Orleans that day.

"It looks really good for the merger, but there are a couple of things I've still got to iron out. I should be back by tomorrow night. Meet me then?"

"I can't, Donovan. I'll be with a client all afternoon and it's sure to run through dinner."

"Damn it, Liz. There's always something."

"I...I can't help it. I told you at the start that my hours were sporadic."

"Yeah, but every time I want to see you you've got something else planned. You're avoiding me, aren't you?"

"We could meet here in the office the morning after you get back."

"How about at the Park Lane for breakfast?"

"Nine-thirty...here?"

"See? You won't do it. Hell, there's nothing I can do in a public restaurant, Liz."

She clicked her tongue. "You're in a temper this morning."

"Damn right, I am. I wanted to be seeing you, not running to New Orleans. Come on, Liz. Make my day. Promise to meet me for breakfast Friday morning. You meet your other clients for meals. Well, I need to consult with you, too, and I'm a busy man. What with the circles you've had me running in for the past few weeks, I've gotten zilch done at the office. It'd save both of us time if we could kill two birds with one stone. Breakfast?"

Feeling unbelievably helpless, Liz nodded. "What time?"

His tone picked up instantly, the words coming faster. "Eight-thirty. Hey, thanks, Liz. I'll look forward to it. See you then."

"Donovan? Have a good trip."

"Thanks, love. So long."

DONOVAN WAS LOOKING bright and chipper when Liz arrived at the Park Lane dining room on Friday morning. They were seated at a round table by the window overlooking Central Park, and their coffee was poured in an instant.

"It's good to see you, Liz."

It was good to see him, too—just how much she tried to ignore. "How did it go in New Orleans?"

"Great. We're on our way."

"Then the deal will go through."

"Looks that way. How've *you* been?"

"Fine. I've got a terrific bunch of articles from the interviews you did on the road," she offered enthusiastically. "Any word yet on the latest sales figures?"

"Not yet. I'm hoping to get a look at them today."

They ordered breakfast, and Liz looked up to find him staring at her. "Don't look at me that way, Donovan."

"What way?"

"*That* way."

"I enjoy looking at you. I feel like I'm finally home."

She rolled her eyes. "Must be all the flying you've been doing. You're still in the clouds."

He grinned. "You bet. Hey, what's the word on Jamie? Is everything okay?"

"For the time being, yes. The girl decided to drop her complaint. Not that she didn't have a case. But Jamie's lawyer was able to convince her that it would cost *both* of them if they were to end up in court. Jamie's agreed to stay away from her, and he knows that if he dares lift a finger again he'll be in real trouble."

"Will the scare work?"

"God, I hope so," Liz said with a sigh. "The lawyer told me he was fully apologetic when he saw Susan."

"Did he sound it to you?"

"Jamie? I don't know. I haven't spoken with him since he left here." She realized how odd that sounded and rushed on. "I didn't want to push things. I'm sure he feels ashamed, and it must be worse when he has to face me."

"But he ran to you when it first happened?"

"He didn't know what to do. He's always run to me like that. I'll talk to him next week, when things have died down."

"Next week's Thanksgiving. Have you made plans?"

She brightened. "I'm going for dinner on Long Island with some friends from the office. One of them has family there and we were all invited. How about you?"

"If you'd been free, I would have stayed here. But since you're deserting me, I guess I'll have to put in an appearance in St. Louis."

Teasing him right back, she eyed him boldly. "Don't give me that 'since you're deserting me' line. I know as well as anyone that you've had to have reservations for months to get on a plane going anywhere for Thanksgiving. It's the busiest time of year at airports."

"Well, I did make reservations early, but I could wangle another if you'd come with me. How about it? You'd like my family."

"I'm sure I would, but I can't go. I told you. I've already got plans."

"With friends. This is something else."

"Oh . . . ?" Liz was steeling herself for a protest when another thought intruded. "Do you see David for the holidays?"

Donovan, too, seemed distracted by the question. "Uh, no. He stays with Ginny and Ron. They mean so much to him. I couldn't ask him to leave."

"Does he know your family?"

"I've taken him to St. Louis a couple of times. It was nice. Well, maybe a little awkward. I mean, the two of us are finally comfortable with one another, but introducing my whole family into the picture is a little overwhelming." He thought for a minute, then shrugged. "Maybe I'm selfish and want him all to myself. Then again, maybe I'm afraid my family will say I'm doing something wrong. I guess I'm not too sure of myself in the role of a father."

"The fact that you recognize it probably makes you a that much better one," she reasoned gently. "It's the parents who take their children for granted who present the real problem. Being born is something none of us asks for."

Donovan studied her intently, then chose his words with care. "Do you think your father regretted having children?"

It took her a long time to answer, and when she did it was a simple, "I don't know." Then she turned the conversation back to him. "Will you be seeing David at all?"

"He's coming east to spend time with me for Christmas. I'm looking forward to it."

"That should be nice."

"I'd like you to meet him."

"You don't need *me* complicating the picture," she said, alluding to his earlier comment.

"You're different. I'd like it. I'll even bring him to the office," he teased in a drawl, "if that'll make you feel better."

Strangely, Liz did want to meet David. "That might be okay."

Their breakfast arrived then, and they set to work eating. It was only as they prepared to leave that Donovan reached into his pocket and withdrew a small box. "Here. This is for you."

Liz stared at the box, then Donovan, then the box again. She was about to protest when he took the wind from her sails.

"It's a pair of earrings I bought in San Francisco. I remembered your saying that you loved buyings things for people, so I decided to give it a try. You were right. I had a ball shopping. Go on. Open the box. I want to know what you think."

For a minute Liz couldn't speak because her throat was tight. She couldn't remember the last time someone had bought her something just for the fun of it. Hands trembling slightly, she slid the ribbon from the box and lifted its lid. Inside, nestled in a bed of cotton, was a pair of solid-gold hoops. They were small but wide, actually three bands joined together, and positively beautiful in their simplicity.

"They're stunning," she breathed.

His face glowed. "You like them?"

"Oh, yes. But you shouldn't have . . . and . . . there's one problem."

"They're for pierced ears. I know. That was what I debated about for the longest time. But your lobes are tiny and just right for piercing, and if you decide not to do it I can have them converted." Actually, what he'd spent the longest time thinking about were the *other* earrings be'd buy her in time. He wanted her to have pearl ones and onyx, and of course, diamonds. Nothing elaborate in design, because that wasn't her style, but simple, and classy, and . . . only from him.

Gazing at the earrings, Liz knew Donovan was right. Her lobe was small, a perfect size for the hoops to curve snugly around. They would be nothing more than a fine gold extension, in no way showy or burdensome.

"I've never thought of having my ears pierced."

"There's nothing to it. I've got a doctor friend who'd do it in a minute."

"I don't know, Donovan." She spoke very softly, her gaze focused on the earrings. "They're so beautiful . . ."

He took her hand then and squeezed it. "Think about it for a while. I'll take you if you want to have your ears pierced. If not, I'll have a jeweler put on a conventional back."

She still didn't look up. "I'm . . . I'm stunned. You didn't have to buy me anything."

"I know. That's what made it so much fun. Will you . . . think about it?" One part of him had been worried that she'd refuse to accept his gift, and he was jubilant that she hadn't.

"Yes." She looked up then, her eyes suspiciously moist. "Thank you. I can't remember when I've ever received anything quite as lovely."

He simply smiled at her, and his own throat was tight. He cleared it after a minute and, putting the lid back on the box, reached down and thrust it into her bag. Then, taking her hand, he led her from the dining room. Neither of them spoke during the short ride to her office, and Donovan continued on in the cab to his own. He was pleased with the breakfast that had just been and sensed that to push Liz to see him the next day, or the day after that, would only be to jeopardize what he felt was building. It was a matter of strategy in a game that meant the world to him. He had to give her time without pressure, time to adapt to their relationship, to realize that it was more than simply a business one. He had to give her time to understand that she could love him, if she wanted, and that he'd never hurt her.

Liz didn't hear from Donovan that weekend. She spent time thinking about the Sunday they'd spent at his house north of Troy, spent time thinking about the closeness she felt toward him, spent time looking at the earrings he'd given her and knowing that she'd cherish them for life.

He dropped by the office on Monday to give her the good news. Preliminary figures showed that the health-food sales, which two weeks before had been in a serious slump, were beginning to pick up. Whether it was Donovan's television appeal or the full-page ads she'd had placed in prominent newspapers that had done it, they weren't sure, but things were looking up, and they were both ecstatic.

On Tuesday there was more good news. An anonymous tip had led federal authorities to a man suspected of poison-dusting Donovan's fields. He was being booked for the two murders. It turned out that Donovan did know the culprit—or had known him once. He was a fellow revolutionary, a psychedelic tripper, an aging hippie who had lashed out at what he perceived to be Donovan's defection to big-time establishment. Though Donovan was deeply dismayed at the thought that people had died because of him, he was nonetheless relieved that the mystery had been solved.

"Today is worth marking," he announced on the phone. "Ill pick you up at the office tonight and we can—"

"I can't, Donovan," Liz broke in before he got carried away. Of the thinking she'd done since the Friday before, a good deal had centered on the ramifications of her accepting his gift. At the time she'd been taken off guard, too pleased to question his motives. Though she still wasn't sure what those were, she knew that, though she'd cherish the earrings always, she had to keep her relationship with him in perspective. "I'm taking the train to Philadelphia for a meeting this afternoon. I'll be back tonight but I don't know when."

"That's okay. You can give me a call before you leave Phillie and I'll meet the train—"

"It'll be late and I'll be exhausted."

He breathed an undisguised sigh of frustration. "And I'm leaving for St. Louis at noontime tomorrow, with a million appointments crammed into the morning. I won't see you before Thanksgiving."

"No," she acknowledged quietly, then waited out a long pause until at last Donovan spoke again.

"I'm sorry about that. I was really hoping...ah, hell, I sometimes wonder..." He seemed to be rolling his dice the wrong way.

There was another pause. This time Liz bit her lip. She didn't want to know what he was hoping, what he sometimes wondered. She sensed she wouldn't like what she learned.

"Okay, Liz. Well, have a nice Thanksgiving."

"You, too, Donovan," she said softly.

"Sure. Talk with you later."

When he hung up the phone, Liz slowly did the same. She knew she'd hurt him, knew that he was annoyed with her, but she couldn't help it. He was going to have to accept the lines she'd drawn. She had her own life, one she'd put together and built through sheer grit. The disappointment she felt right now would be nothing, she knew, compared with the anguish she'd suffer later if she let Donovan have his way.

Yet there was guilt. Always guilt. She liked Donovan so much, and it hurt her to hurt him. She thought about him during the train ride to Philadelphia and back, then long into the night, and was still thinking about him when she was at her desk, supposedly working, on Wednesday morning.

That afternoon she had her ears pierced.

6

"ELIZABETH?"

"Donovan! Perfect timing. I just walked in." She was taking her coat off even as she talked, and she was grinning broadly.

"Happy Thanksgiving."

"Same to you."

"Did you have a nice dinner?"

"It was great. There were eighteen of us, including Sheila's parents and family. They're wonderful people. How about you? Good dinner?"

"My sister cooked . . . or tried. The turkey was dry, the peas were all wrinkled and the lemon soufflé collapsed."

"Poor baby."

"I have to admit it was fun, though. It's nice seeing everyone."

"The nieces and nephews are all well?" Liz knew that though Donovan's sister hadn't married, his brother had. He and his wife had five young children.

"Oh, yeah. Noisy as hell, but terrific. I wish you were here, though. It would be icing on the cake."

"On the sunken soufflé, you mean," she teased.

"No, that's not what I mean. I was thinking of the magnificent pecan pie that I brought to the feast. Funny thing about pecan pies. They're not as elaborate to look at as some fancy desserts, but, man, do they ever taste good."

Liz was too high-spirited to give thought to any message there might have been in his words. "They're very fattening. You'd better watch it, Donovan. Wouldn't want to put on weight."

"I ran five miles this morning. You sound happy."

"I am."

"Tell me one of the eighteen people at your friend's house was a gorgeous guy who bowled you over."

"Not quite."

"Then a homely guy who bowled you over."

She grinned. "Nope. I just feel good. That's all." She wasn't about to say that her spirits had soared with his call, much less admit it to herself.

"Then I'm glad. What are your plans for tomorrow?"

"I'll be working."

"Come on, Liz. Everyone takes the day after Thanksgiving off."

"Which is why I'm going in. Half of the office is out of town, and we've got to have some kind of skeletal staff there to cover."

"So you volunteered. I bet it'll be dead as anything."

"Probably, in which case I'll be able to catch up on my own work."

"You're a glutton for punishment."

"Not punishment. It'll be fun. Very relaxed. And quiet. I like days like those."

"You would," he muttered, but she knew his grudging tone was put on, for it vanished with his next breath. "I'll let you go, then. I'm glad you had a nice day."

"Same here. Thanks for calling, Donovan."

"My pleasure."

HE CALLED HER at the office the following afternoon, just to give her something to do, he explained, then again at home that night, when she was in her night-gown getting ready for bed.

"I'm flying back tomorrow," he began quickly.

"Oh? Is something wrong?"

"Yeah. I want to see you."

"Donovan—"

"A date. Tomorrow night."

"But we—"

"Have a business relationship? We've *had* that. But you've done what I hired you to do, so now it's time to move on. Or haven't you thought about that?"

"I've thought about it," she said softly.

"Good. Because from here on in, we're something else." He'd decided, among other things, that it was time to shift tactics. Her game had been to stall, and as game master, he wanted to move on.

"We're friends."

"That, too. But I want more."

Liz closed her eyes. She'd known it was coming. Donovan just didn't give up. She'd sensed he was bid-ing his time, and she could hear from the impatience in his tone that the biding had taken its toll.

"There's no point," she whispered.

"This connection stinks. I can't hear you."

"I said," she raised her voice, "that there's no point. I've already told you that I don't play your way."

"I'm not talking play. I'm dead serious."

"So am I. If we can't be friends and leave it at that, I guess we'll have to go our separate ways."

"Is that what you want—to go separate ways?"

"No, it's not what I want," she cried. "I want to be friends. But I can't give you anything more."

There was a momentary silence from the other end of the line, then a more gentle, "What're you afraid of, Liz? I won't hurt you. I've told you that before. I've tried to prove it to you by taking things slow. I haven't pushed you lately, have I?"

"No. But you're pushing me now."

"That's because I've been sitting here for two full days thinking of nothing but how much nicer it would be if you were here, if we were together. I want you, Liz. Don't you know that?"

"You don't want me. Not really. You've just built something up in your mind, a challenge you're convinced you've got to meet. But I'm not a challenge. I don't have anything to offer—"

"Christ, we're going in circles. Look, I guess it was a mistake trying to talk this out over the phone. If I was there with you, I'd *show* you what you have to offer. I'm flying in tomorrow and I'll be at your place by seven."

"I won't be here."

"Where *will* you be?"

"That's none of your business." When she heard him grunt she relented. "I'm going to a party." It was a cocktail party at Cheryl Obermeyer's home. Actually she'd been on the fence about going, but it seemed the perfect out now.

"When will you be back?"

"Late. Please, Donovan, leave well enough alone."

"What we've got *isn't* well enough.

"For me it is. Good night, Donovan."

"Damn it, Liz. I want—"

She hung up on him before he could say what he wanted. She knew what it was, and she wouldn't—she just couldn't—give it to him.

AND SO SATURDAY NIGHT found her at the cocktail party she'd rather have skipped. It wasn't that she disliked parties. She enjoyed being with friends and the Obermeyers always welcomed her with open arms. Unfortunately, though, their parties were gathering places for one beautiful couple after another. By contrast, Liz felt conspicuously single and distinctly outclassed.

"I want to talk to you," Cheryl drawled leading her away from the group on whose fringes she'd been standing for what had seemed hours. "You look subdued."

"I'm not. Actually, I'm feeling rather good."

"That's because you've had . . . how many drinks?"

"Just two."

"Which is more than you usually have. And since the first goes right to your head, you probably *are* tipsy, which makes your somber expression that much more mystifying. Something's bothering you."

"Nah. Everything's fine." She lifted her glass to her lips and would have taken a healthy swallow of whatever it was the bartender had handed her. But Cheryl removed the glass from her fingers and set it on a passing tray.

"Talk to me, Liz. You've helped me out when I've needed you. Now it's my turn. And don't tell me nothing's wrong. I know you too well. Your mind has been on anything but this party tonight."

"I'm sorry, Cheryl. I didn't mean—"

"I'm not offended. Just worried. Friends have a right to be that way once in a while, y' know?"

"I know. And I appreciate it, really I do, but—"

"Who is he?"

"He?"

"Whatever man it is you're thinking about. That's the only conclusion I can come to. I'm only annoyed that you didn't bring him here."

"Uh . . . it's not like that."

"What is it like?"

Later Liz would blame her loose tongue on liquor. But for the moment she was beyond anything but sharing her woes with Cheryl, who was so very willing to listen and give advice. "He's a client. His name's Donovan Grant."

Cheryl gave a low whistle. "Donovan Grant. The DIG Group. Didn't I see him on television recently?"

"That was part of the work I did for him. We're trying to counter the adverse effect on sales—"

"Of health foods. I know the case. All the time I was reading about it, I kept wondering what *we'd* do if our customers suddenly developed a rash from a lethal something that was used in the manufacture of our clothes. They've caught the guy who did it, though, thank God. Donovan Grant. Now there's a super catch. Gorgeous, and from what I've read, he mans four very profitable divisions—"

"Six, actually. And he's about to take over the Ullman conglomerate in New Orleans."

Cheryl's eyes widened, then darted from Liz and narrowed on her brother, who had sidled up sometime during the conversation. "We're having a private discussion, Raymond. You can talk with Liz later." Tightening her grip on Liz's elbow, she inched her farther away from the other guests. "Donovan Grant is one very shrewd businessman. And available. So he's the one who's got you in a dither?"

Liz nodded, her expression pained.

"Have you two been dating?"

"Not . . . really. Well, maybe you could call it dating, but he wants more and I'm not sure I do, and it bothers me. I don't want to hurt him. He's really a wonderful guy."

"Why ever wouldn't you want to date him?"

Given her light head, Liz had to struggle all the more to express herself. "He's too good and too successful and too handsome. He's everything I'm not. We're poorly matched."

"I wouldn't think so, and neither must he, if he's the one who's doing the chasing."

"That's just it. It's a game. He's big with things like that. But I'm not. I take life more seriously."

"Maybe you shouldn't. I mean, maybe you should let him chase you and see where it leads."

"I'll only be hurt in the process. What do I need it for, Cheryl? I've got a good life, a good career."

"So do I, but I'd give my right arm for a good man. Don't you ever sit back and picture yourself ten or twenty years down the road? I do and I'm not sure I like what I see. I'll have poured blood and sweat into the business, and to what end?"

"You'll be well respected and wealthy."

"Sure, I'll be wealthy, but if I've got no one to share it with, what good is it? Okay, maybe wealth isn't your thing. What will *you* have?"

Liz forced a grin. "This is getting too serious for me. I can't think straight."

"You're just avoiding the issue."

"No, really . . ."

"Okay, I'll let you off the hook for now. But think about it later. Think about what I've said. If you decide then that you still don't want Donovan Grant," she said grinning slyly, "give him my number." With that, Cheryl eased Liz back into the mainstream of the party.

It was, ironically, those last words and their accompanying grin that stuck most in Liz's mind. Though she'd never have imagined herself capable of it, she felt distinct jealousy when she pictured Cheryl with Donovan. That jealousy shocked and disappointed her so much that when Donovan showed up unannounced at her front door on Sunday, she was spoiling for a fight.

"Back to your old tricks?" she said, standing aside to let him in. She was dressed this time in slacks and a sweater, and hadn't even bothered to tell him to go away.

Donovan shrugged. "There's always someone going in or out of this building. If the downstairs door's wide open, what can I do?"

"You could have buzzed up anyway."

"And you would have told me to get lost."

"Not this time. This time we've got to talk."

But he was staring at her, then a slow smile spread over his face. His voice was suddenly as gentle as his expression. "You had yours ears pierced."

Liz found herself melting. It happened whenever he looked at her that way. Almost shyly, she fingered one earlobe. "I . . . I decided the earrings were too beautiful to sit in a drawer."

"When did you do it?"

"Wednesday."

"You should have waited for me. I would have taken you."

"I would have been embarrassed. I'm not terribly good when it comes to pain."

He was touching her ear ever so lightly, his fingers brushing, lingering against hers. "Tell me they had to strap you down."

"No. But I practically passed out."

"You didn't."

"I did. The nurse made me stay at the office for a whole hour afterward before she'd let me go."

"It doesn't hurt now, does it?"

She shook her head, unable to speak with Donovan so close, so dear, his body so vibrantly stirring her own.

"They look great," he murmured, pushing aside her hair and touching the upper curve of her ear with his lips.

She wanted to tell him not to do it, but the words wouldn't come because his breath was warm, sending shivers of heat through her, and his hands whispered over her back, and she felt good, so good, and cherished. So she told herself she'd enjoy this last bit of heaven before she put it behind her.

She didn't object when he murmured soft words of encouragement against her cheek or when his hands left her back to skim her thighs, her ribs, her breasts, or even when he framed her face and tipped it up. His lips opened, dusting her eyes, her nose, her chin, and she was waiting when they finally teased her own with the same airy ghost of a kiss. Needing firmer contact, she tried to catch him, but his mouth eluded hers and continued its tantalizing butterfly play.

"Donovan," she moaned, clutching his wrists, "you're torturing me."

He hummed a smile against her cheek, then ended the torment and seized her lips with a force that stole what little breath she had. His mouth slanted and sucked. He thrust his tongue deeply and she willingly received it. She was ravaged and devoured, but felt more whole than ever before.

When at last he tore his lips from hers, his body was a mass of coiled sexuality. "This is what I've needed, what I've missed," he growled, holding her face and looking into her eyes. "Tell me it's not the same for you."

If only he hadn't spoken . . . thank God he'd spoken! Liz blinked once before she registered his words and the look of intent on his face. She opened her mouth to speak but her throat was knotted. He wanted to make love to her. Unmistakably. Urgently. She began to shake, but not in passion.

He gripped her shoulders as she tried to ease back. "Oh, no. Don't back out on me now, Liz!"

"I have to," she whispered.

"Damn it, you don't!"

"I never promised you this, Donovan. All along I've been telling you I didn't want it."

"Your body tells me differently. And so does mine, damn it!" But he saw the fear in her eyes, and it quickly dulled his physical drive. He held up both hands and stepped back. "Okay. You said you wanted to talk. Let's talk." Turning, he walked to the sofa and settled into it with his arm along its back and one knee crossed over the other. Though his pose was casual, his expression was anything but.

Liz stood clutching her hands in front of her for a minute, then slowly walked to the window. She stood staring out with her back to him and began to speak quietly.

"I've led a very different life from you, Donovan. I never rebelled. I never sowed any wild oats. And I never wanted to. What I wanted was a secure life, a life where I was the one in control. I wanted freedom, but a freedom to do what *I* wanted, *when* I wanted it, even if that all fell along very conventional lines." She took a deep breath. "I've never included a man in that vision."

"That's what I don't understand," Donovan stated. "If you're as conventional as all that, there's got to be a husband and kids somewhere in the picture. Isn't that the meaning of security?"

She turned slowly and rested back against the sill. "It's one meaning. For some women. But not for me. I define security as self-determination. I *choose* to lead the life I do, and I'm happy that way."

"But you're not a hermit. You do have friends. Friends who depend on you, who ask things of you. You help one by baby sitting when she and her husband need time alone. You help another out by talking with her brother when he starts to act up. It's not a question of being selfish."

"I never said it was. But I'm free. I can pick and choose what I want to do. I can pick and choose the context in which I want to do it. If something is too uncomfortable or threatening, I don't have to do it."

"And the thought of a relationship with me makes you uncomfortable. It threatens you."

"Yes."

"But *why*? That's what I don't understand."

"You wouldn't. You've always been on top of the heap." When he opened his mouth to object, she rushed on. "Anything you've done, you've done well. Even when you were a revolutionary, as you call it, you were respected and admired. I never had that, Donovan. Growing up, I was an outcast. I was shy and withdrawn. I didn't have friends to speak of, because I couldn't begin to compete with the other kids. Oh, yes, I could be a follower. I could tag along with the group until they got tired of me and left me by the wayside. But I didn't want that. It hurt too much. So I stayed by myself until I got through college and into graduate school. It was only then that I met more accepting people."

"Hell, you talk as if you've got leprosy or something," he sneered, looking away.

"Not leprosy. But I can't run in the fast lane. I can't keep up. I'm still shy. Okay, I've learned to handle myself professionally; and socially to an extent. But that's because I *do* pick and choose those professional and social situations."

There was a long silence while Donovan gnawed on his lip. He looked up with an abruptness that momentarily shook Liz. "So what's this got to do with me? With us?"

"Don't you see? I can't keep up with you. You're suave and sophisticated. You're good-looking and personable. You can handle yourself in any and every situation that crosses your path. *I* could never have faced those interviewers or those television cameras. It's one thing to understand what's needed for things like that, and I do, which is why I could talk with you beforehand and prepare you. But to be on the firing line myself . . . I'd wither."

"Not everyone can be on the firing line. And I may have looked like Mr. Cool during those interviews, but my stomach did its share of jumping."

"Still, you *thrive* on new adventures, new challenges. I don't. I want things gentle and manageable."

"You constantly face challenges in your work."

"But it's all within a context I know I can handle. Do you remember when we were talking last Thursday and I said I was looking forward to working on Friday? Well, I was. The office, for me, is a haven. It's something I know, something I can manage. Sure, problems crop up all the time. But there are guidelines to follow, and there are other people, people I can trust, to give me advice."

"I'm sure you give *them* advice as often. Damn it, Liz, why do you keep putting yourself down? You've convinced yourself that you're this little wilting daisy, and it just isn't so."

"Isn't it? I'm nothing to look at. You can do better in a minute."

He groaned and rolled his head to the side. "Here we go again." Then he met her gaze squarely. "I've never had any problem with your looks, Liz. You're the only one who's hung up on it."

"I'm a realist," she returned crossly. "I know what my limits are."

"But what about stretching them? What about growing?" His eyes widened for a fleeting instant. "I mean, maybe I'm missing something here. You do like me, don't you?"

"Yes. I like you. You've been a more agreeable client than some—"

"Forget client. Think person. Better still, think man. Do you like me?"

"As a person, yes."

"And as a man?"

"I . . . I don't want to think of you that way."

"Because you *do* like me that way and it scares you."

"That's not the point," she countered, eyes flashing. "If I chose not to look at you in sexual terms, it's my right!"

"But you're fighting it," he said more softly. "You *do* see me in sexual terms, and you're fighting it. I want to know why."

"I don't want sex."

"Why?"

"Because . . . I don't."

"I thought you wanted to talk, Liz, but you're not doing it. You happen to be the most thoughtful, understanding person I know. Why can't you turn that strength toward yourself and express your feelings to me?"

Liz knew they'd reached an impasse and she grew more frustrated than ever. "Because they're *my* feelings and I choose not to express them!"

Donovan stared at her thoughtfully, absently rubbing his upper lip. She held her breath, wondering where he'd go from here. Of all the directions she imagined him taking, she wasn't prepared for the one he did.

"I've given this lots of thought, Liz. Lots of thought. You're open to a relationship, but only to the point of sex. You back off then, and with pure terror. You say that you're a virgin, that there haven't been any men in your life, but you're terrified, and there's got to be cause. It's my guess that your father abused you."

For a minute Liz couldn't answer, but only for a minute. "He did not! He never once raised a hand against me!"

"There are many different kinds of abuse, some of which don't involve physical force."

"You're way out of line, Donovan!" she cried. "And it's because you're too bullheaded to believe that I don't want you in my life. I've been saying it from the first, but you've refused to listen. Because it's all a game to you! All a game!"

"Hold on now," he gritted, rising from his seat and approaching her. "I'm not bullheaded, and if you assume that a game implies I'm just toying with you, you're wrong. I'm dead serious about my interest in you." Liz was backed to the window and he was within arm's reach. "Is that what's got you worried? That I'll love you and leave you?"

She scrunched up her face and squeezed her eyes shut. "I don't *want* you to love me! You're not listening! I don't want any *part* of you!"

"No?" He reached for her, but she twisted to the side and ran to the door, swinging it open with a flourish.

"Get out, Donovan." Her voice shook, though her entire body was stiff. "I don't need you, and I don't want you."

He was beside her in an instant, slamming the door shut again with one hand. "I don't believe you. I think you're just scared. You're nearly thirty years old, Liz. Isn't it about time you grew up?"

"Get out," she repeated, this time through gritted teeth. When he didn't budge, she was livid. "So help me, I'll call the police."

"You wouldn't do that. You like me too much."

"I *don't* like you!" she yelled. "You're an arrogant bastard who thinks he knows everything. Well, you don't, buster. You don't know what I—" she prodded her chest with her forefinger "—think. *I* think that you're thick. *Thick*! Liberal—hah! You're one of the most narrow-minded people I've had the misfortune to meet, because you can't accept the fact that someone else sees differently from you. You play games and they're cruel! You'd stamp all over me if you had the chance, because you're so damned sure that you know what's best! Well, you don't!" Her chest was rising and falling rapidly with the labored working of her lungs. "And who are *you* to tell me what to do with my life? You blew it with your son, because you just couldn't accept the responsibility!" When he recoiled as though he'd been slapped, she gloated. "And you're nearly *forty* and only now thinking of all you've missed."

She took a gasping breath and narrowed her eyes. "So don't tell me what I should or shouldn't be doing. You might be the idol of the business world, but in *my* world, you're nothing! Do you hear me? *Nothing!*"

Donovan's face was pale and for a minute he said nothing. Then he spoke slowly, distinctly. "I hear you. For all else I may be, I'm not deaf." Lowering his hand, he pulled the door open. He turned on the threshold to look at her a final time, but his eyes were hard. "I won't bother you again. Goodbye, Elizabeth."

It was all she could do to hold her head high until she'd shut the door on him. Then she sagged back against it and closed her eyes, taking long, shuddering breaths. A minute later she pushed herself from the door, and, in a flurry, raced to the kitchen for a dust rag.

The apartment, bathroom and all, was gleaming by the time she'd finished, and still she looked around for more to do. On impulse, she dashed into her bedroom and changed into a skirt, then threw on her coat and headed for the nearest museum. There she stared at one painting after another until she had a headache.

In search of fresh air, she went outside and started walking, aimlessly but at a rapid pace. She kept her hands buried deep in her pockets because she'd not thought to bring gloves and the late November chill seemed to penetrate her very being. She bought a bag of roasted chestnuts from a corner vendor, but she seemed to have lost her knack for removing the shells, for they ended up more often than not in her mouth. Finally she tossed the bag in the nearest trash can and ducked, instead, into a coffee shop.

Neither hot coffee nor steaming chowder made a dent in the chill she felt. But she couldn't bear the thought of returning to her apartment, and she couldn't think of anyone she wanted to visit, so she began walking again. When she passed a theater, she doubled back, bought a ticket and went inside. There, with a large buttered popcorn propped in her lap, she sat. And watched. Or tried to watch. Her mind kept wandering, to the point that once, when the background music rose abruptly, she jumped in alarm and spilled the entire bucket of popcorn onto her skirt and the floor. Flustered, she tried to brush it off, but her embarrassment only increased when she found the motion attracting the attention of those around her. Grateful only for the dark of the theater which would surely hide her true identity from any who might wonder, she pulled herself together, ignoring a snicker, and left.

Dusk was beginning to fall, but she walked on. And on. Finally, she found herself on the edge of Central Park. Exhausted by now, she collapsed onto a bench facing Fifth Avenue. Cars passed and taxis and limousines. She watched their progression, wondering who was inside and where they were headed, until she realized that she just didn't care. *They* didn't care. They were strangers, people with their own lives, their own destinations. They wouldn't even notice her, sitting alone on her bench.

It was then that her eyes filled with tears. Slowly they trickled down her cold cheeks and then her nose began to run. Liz dug into her purse for a Kleenex, which she pressed to her lips to muffle the quiet sobs. She couldn't seem to stop. Yes, she was alone. She was alone, and by choice. And for the first time in her life she regretted it. For the first time in her life she felt truly lonely.

"THAT WAS A REALLY DUMB thing to do," Karen informed her after Liz had poured out her heart the following Thursday morning. "You could have been mugged, or worse, raped, sitting by the park at night that way."

"I think I would have welcomed it at the time. *Anything* for human contact."

"You should have called me . . . or come over. I was home all day Sunday."

"Alone?" Liz prompted, knowing the answer.

"Well, David was there, but he would have understood if we'd had to talk."

"I couldn't talk then. I couldn't think. I just felt so . . . so numb. . . . Not numb because I was freezing, but numb *inside* . . . do you know what I mean?" She looked down. "I'm even amazed that I've talked now."

"You talked because I dragged you in here and demanded that you explain why you've been a walking zombie all week."

"That bad?" Liz asked timidly.

"That bad. Well, maybe not so obvious to someone who doesn't know you and care, but I'm not the only one who's been concerned. Julie and Veronica approached me individually, and I know that Donna's worried, too." She donned a mischievous grin. "They're convinced you're pregnant."

"They are not."

"So, what are you going to do about it?"

"About not being pregnant?"

"About Donovan. Do you love him?"

"*Love* him! You haven't been listening to me. What I feel has nothing to *do* with love. I just feel . . . awful for having said such terrible things to him." Her voice dropped. "And I'm sorry to have lost him as a friend."

"Do you want to see him and apologize?"

Liz thought about that for a minute, but she'd thought about it before and had ruled it out for the same reasons she now gave Karen. "It wouldn't do any good, other than to ease my conscience. Some words you can't take back. Apology or no, I'll always hear myself saying them. I'm sure Donovan will, too. And if he doesn't, and I apologize, he's apt to think the game is on again, and I don't want that."

"Are you sure? Isn't there some small part of you that's upset to have lost Donovan . . . for other reasons?"

"No. Definitely no."

"You say that with such conviction. Almost too much."

"Then blame it on the past week. I'm telling you, Karen, I don't want what he wants. It's as simple as that. Regrettably, I had to say a lot of ugly things to get Donovan to believe it, but now that he does, I'm relieved."

"Could have fooled me," Karen mumbled, then pulled herself up and took a breath. "Okay. The ques-

tion is where do I go from here. I got a call this morning from a greeting card company in Kansas City that
wants us to do some work for them. It'd mean a trip out
there . . . as soon as possible. I think what you need to
pick up your spirits is a change of scenery. Does it
sound . . . appealing?"

"Right on the button," Liz responded, brightening for
the first time in days. "If I clean up some things this afternoon, I could be on my way tomorrow morning."

"Good. Why don't you plan on it, then. I'll call Kansas City and let them know you're coming. My secretary will type up the specifics of the case and get them
to you. You won't work through the weekend, though,
will you?"

Liz was on her feet, revived by the thought of a new
case, a new city. "Nah. I'll just wander around. I can
work tomorrow, then as many days next week as I have
to. Since there's nothing pressing here, it'll work out
well."

Karen walked her to the door. "I hope it does . . . for
you. I, well, I was really hoping things would work out
with Donovan, but I've never been one to beat a dead
horse. I want you to be happy, Liz. You know that, don't
you?"

"I do, Karen. And thanks." On impulse Liz gave her
a hug, then headed for her office to make arrangements for the trip.

SHE LEFT FOR KANSAS CITY the following morning and
spent a relatively relaxing five days away from New
York, getting to know a new client and its product, letting the wounds of the past days heal. Though she con-

tinued to be bothered by the things she'd said to Donovan, she became more and more convinced that the outcome was for the best. If she'd lost one friend, she had others. It was time to pick up where she'd left off on that day she'd flown to Troy.

If she assumed that Reynolds Associates had completed its work for the DIG Group, though, she'd been mistaken. It seemed that Donovan had decided to retain the firm to do future publicity on the merger with Ullman. At his request Liz had been removed from the account.

7

"GOT A MINUTE, LIZ?"

Liz looked up quickly from her work to find Brenda Nussbaum at her door. She smiled and sat back. "Sure, Brenda. Come on in."

"Am I interrupting anything urgent?"

"I was just going over some of the figures I brought back with me from Kansas City. I want to get the ball rolling on this thing." It had been over a week since she'd been back, and only during the past few days had she felt she was working up to par.

"Is there a problem?"

"Just piles of figures to wade through. The annual reports this company has put out in the past leave something to be desired."

"That's why they hired you, I'm sure."

"Us. They hired us."

Brenda slipped into a seat, looking decidedly sheepish. "Yeah, well, I'm glad you feel that way, because *I* need your help. And since the DIG Group hired *us* . . ."

"Uh-oh." Liz's easy smile faded. "What's wrong?"

Brenda threw a hand in the air and shook her head. "It's Donovan Grant. I don't understand him. How a man could come across as being so congenial, so easy-going in the press and turn out to be a man of stone in person mystifies me."

"Man of stone?"

"Exactly. Oh, he always says and does the right things, but he's so . . . so formal about it."

"Formal?"

"I mean, I think he's the best thing to come along since Robert Redford. All he has to do is to walk into the room and my heart starts pounding." She looked up from pleating her skirt. "I suppose I shouldn't be telling you this . . . or even feeling it, for that matter. . . and I know that a professional relationship should be just that, and I'm ready to settle for it if only he'd let me."

Liz felt her own heart pound. "He's coming on to you?"

"Just the opposite. He insists on my coming to his office, and when I dare suggest, even innocently, that we might discuss something over lunch or dinner he all but turns me into ice with those eyes of his." She was frowning. "I thought you might be able to give me some hints."

"Hints . . . on what?" There was a sudden chill in Liz's voice, but she was unaware of it. Brenda wasn't.

"Uh-oh. I've offended you. You must think I'm awful. Oh, Liz, I'm sorry."

"You haven't offended me. I'm just not sure what it is you want."

"I want a comfortable working relationship with him. I mean, it'd be nice if he'd notice me as a woman, but I can only do so much. I agonize over what I'm going to wear on the days I see him. I make sure I don't eat anything with garlic in it for lunch. I rack my brain trying to come up with novel ways to present the Ullman merger to the public. And he takes it all in, then quickly ushers me to the door."

Liz was amazed. Brenda was young, redheaded, adorable and available. If Donovan had wanted a playmate, she was his for the asking. But he wasn't asking. And now Brenda had come to her for advice. How do you tell a girl that the game was only fun if the object was unadorable, inexperienced and disinterested, and therein lay the challenge?

"You've worked with him, Liz. Was he that way with you?"

Liz felt a bitter laugh bubbling but squelched it. It was really ludicrous, a first, that a woman as appealing as Brenda should come to one as unappealing as herself and innocently ask how a man had been with her. On the other hand, maybe Brenda needed the reassurance that it wasn't just her, and who better to come to than the ugly duckling of the firm?

"He...had his moments. But I think he's very wrapped up in the Ullman thing and—"

"You can say that again! You'd think his entire future depended on this acquisition. He put me through the second degree yesterday because some idiot is suddenly buying huge chunks of Ullman stock. Just because the guy's family is one of our clients—"

"Whoa. What did you say?"

"I met with Donovan at his office yesterday and he all but accused me of selling inside information to another client."

"Which client?"

"The Obermeyers. Actually, it's the son, Raymond, who's been snatching up stock in Ullman, at least that's what Donovan's sources claim."

For a minute Liz couldn't breathe. "It's a federal crime to pass on inside information like that," she murmured. "Whoever buys stock just prior to a merger stands to make a bundle as soon as the merger is announced."

"That's what Donovan said. I assured him that we don't discuss one client with another, but I'm not sure he believed me. He seems to think I'm pretty raw in this business."

She was, though Liz wouldn't have said so. Brenda, evidently, didn't realize that the Obermeyers were *Liz's* clients. But the more Liz thought about it, the more uncomfortable she grew. It could be a coincidence, Ray's buying Ullman stock. On the other hand, there'd been that cocktail party after Thanksgiving . . . and Liz had had one too many...and she'd talked with Cheryl. What *had* she said . . .

"I don't know, Liz. Am I doing something wrong?"

"Uh-uh, Bren," she answered distractedly. "You're doing just fine. Bear with Donovan. He tends to be intense about some things. It must be a trying time for him."

"God, I hope that's all." She talked on a little longer about what she planned to do to publicize the Ullman merger, and Liz nodded from time to time. Then she stood up and shook her head as she started for the door. "Another Redford . . . just slipping through my fingers . . ."

Fortunately Brenda didn't look back, because Liz wasn't smiling. Her heart was pounding, and it wasn't even Donovan she was thinking of at that moment. Lifting the phone, she called Cheryl Obermeyer.

"I have to see you, Cheryl. Can we meet somewhere for lunch?"

"You sound uptight. What's wrong?"

"I . . . I can't talk about it now. Can we meet?"

"Sure, but not until two o'clock."

"That's fine."

Cheryl named a place they'd been to together several times before, and Liz hung up the phone feeling that at least she'd taken the first step. She accomplished nothing between then and two, though, because thought of the steps to follow had her tied up in knots. She waited until she and Cheryl had been seated before broaching the subject.

"Cheryl, do you remember that night at your party when we were talking?"

"Of course." She grinned. "You were a mite tipsy and told me all about Donovan Grant."

"What 'all' did I tell you?"

"Just that he wanted to date you and that you didn't want to."

"Did I say anything about his business interests?"

Cheryl was no longer grinning, because she couldn't help but sense Liz's distress. "I don't remember. Why? What's this all about?"

With a grimace, Liz hung her head. When she looked up again, there was a pleading slant to her eyes. "I . . . I think I told you something I shouldn't have. Something about a merger."

With the prompting Cheryl remembered. She frowned, struggling to draw back the facts. "Mmm. With the Ullman Distributorship, wasn't it?" Liz nodded. "Well?"

"Someone has been buying Ullman stock in bulk. I believe it's Ray."

"Ray? But how could he...he wouldn't..." Her eyes widened. "Oh dear. He was right behind you when you told me. He must have heard."

It was all the confirmation Liz needed to support her suspicion. "I was hoping I was wrong. I've been trying to dredge up every detail of that conversation since I learned of the problem this morning. I kept thinking Ray's sudden interest in Ullman was a coincidence. But he *did* hear me that night. And we both know he'd be tempted."

"He would, damn his soul. Liz, who knows about this?"

"Donovan does."

"Did he accuse you?"

She shook her head. "We're not working together anymore."

"You're kidding. Why not?"

"I can't go into it, Cheryl. There's too much else we have to worry about. I learned about the stock business by accident, in the course of a discussion with the woman who's now working with Donovan. She said he's livid."

"Has he made the connection between you and Ray?"

"No. Neither did she. I called you as soon as she left my office."

"Thank God you did," Cheryl murmured, frowning down at her plate. "We've got to figure out the best thing to do. Damn it, both you *and* Ray could be in serious legal trouble if something's not done." She put her hand on Liz's. "You weren't really hungry, were you? It'd be best if I got back to the office and spoke with our lawyer."

"And Ray."

"Right . . . damn him. How could he do this?"

"Maybe he's trying to get back at me for having cajoled him into staying put."

"Maybe, but I doubt it. I doubt he'd put his own neck on the line just to spite you. On the other hand, he may be too dumb to realize what he's done. He's probably only thinking of the profit he'll make and what he'll be able to do with it." She grabbed her purse and stood. "I'll get back to you as soon as I know anything, okay?"

"I'd appreciate it, Cheryl. I'll be a nervous wreck until you do."

Cheryl bent low for a final minute. "You relax. If push comes to shove, I'll testify that you didn't intentionally divulge privileged information. No one will be able to prove intent, and that's what counts in cases like these."

Liz's smile was weak. "I'd like to believe that, but . . ."

Cheryl patted her arm. "I'll get back to you."

"Thanks."

LIZ SAT THROUGH a long afternoon and an even longer evening at the office waiting for Cheryl's call, but it didn't come. Finally she went home, knowing that Cheryl would call her there if she had anything to report. By morning, though, when there was still no word, Liz knew that she had to do something else. Dressing carefully, she stopped in at the office for only the time it took to postpone two appointments, then she headed for DIG headquarters.

Donovan was in Troy, but was expected back before noon, she was told. She decided to wait, fearing that if she left she'd lose her nerve and never return. And, she reasoned, the longer the receptionist saw her sitting there, the harder it would be to run out, which was what she wanted to do more than anything else in the world at that moment. It would have been difficult enough three weeks before, to confess to Donovan what she'd done. But now, given what had happened, given what she'd said to him the last time they'd seen each other, it was a truly terrifying prospect.

By eleven-thirty, when Donovan walked past her into the reception area, she was pale and tense. The receptionist smiled in greeting, then shifted her gaze to Liz. Only then did he turn. His surprise was momentary and was quickly checked, as was the relief that surged through him.

When he'd seen Liz last, she'd hurt him with her words—until he realized that she'd struck out in self-defense. She'd been running scared from his feelings and, more importantly, from her own. He'd realized then that he had to wait for her to come to him, and he'd reminded himself of that each time he'd lifted the phone to call her.

It was her turn. She had the dice in her hand. All he could do was to patiently wait for her to roll them and make her move.

"Did you want to see me?" he asked evenly.

She prayed for as even a tone, but only managed a slightly timid, "If you've got a minute."

He hesitated, then gave a short nod. She rose and preceded him to his office, where he closed the door and went straight to his desk. "What is it, Liz?" He thumbed through his mail, then tossed it down and leaned back in his seat. It was all he could do not to round the desk and take her in his arms, but he knew that wouldn't help her. He had to wait.

"I've . . . got a problem."

He shrugged. "Why are you coming to me?"

"Because it concerns you. It's about the Ullman merger." She saw alertness flicker through his otherwise controlled gaze.

"What about it?"

"I've made an awful mistake. I didn't mean to do it, and I didn't realize I'd even done it at the time—"

"Sit down, Liz, and spit it out."

She knew then that he wouldn't make things any easier for her, that she couldn't expect any of the warmth, the gentle understanding that had once seemed such an integral part of his nature. She also knew that she'd accomplish nothing by hedging. She looked at him and swallowed, awkwardly settled on the edge of the chair facing his desk, then summoned every bit of her inner strength and spoke.

"I went to a cocktail party—maybe you remember—the Saturday night after Thanksgiving. It was at Cheryl Obermeyer's. Cheryl and I are close, and on occasion I've been to family affairs with her. This wasn't exactly a family thing, though, and I felt a little out of the place. I had had two drinks before Cheryl dragged me aside and wanted to know what was bothering me. She could see that I was distracted." Liz looked down. "And I was. In the, uh, process of conversation I mentioned you, and Cheryl went on about how successful you are, and very carelessly I mentioned Ullman." She waited for Donovan to say something. When he didn't, she looked up. "I didn't even realize I'd betrayed your confidence because I was a little fuzzy-headed, and anyway, Cheryl would never have done anything with the information."

"Someone did," Donovan stated somberly. Somehow he hadn't expected this.

"Ray did. Cheryl's brother. He'd come up from behind, and I didn't even know he was there until Cheryl told him to get lost. By then it was too late. Honestly, Donovan, I would never have even mentioned your name if I'd known he was listening." She focused on her fingers, which were kneading her purse. "I don't think he was there long, but he obviously heard enough."

A muscle flexed in Donovan's jaw. Yes, he was angry that Liz had been the one to betray him, yet he couldn't sustain his anger long. She'd come to him on her own with the truth. Perhaps it was the move he needed to force her hand. "He's been buying Ullman stock."

"I know."

"Do you know that given the upcoming merger that's a federal offense?" Germs of an idea were taking shape.

"Yes."

"And that you're as guilty as he is?"

"I didn't do it intentionally—"

"But you did it," he said. "You passed on inside information. For all I know you may be getting a cut in Obermeyer's profit." He knew it wasn't true, but he had to push. He had to know exactly where he stood...and he was buying time to plan his strategy.

"I'm not! I told you, I didn't know anything about this until Brenda mentioned it yesterday. She didn't even realize that the Obermeyers were my clients."

She blotted her dry lips together, a nervous gesture. "As soon as Brenda left I called Cheryl, and we met yesterday afternoon. She's as upset as I am. She promised to speak to her lawyer and to Ray, then get back to me. But I haven't heard from her." She threw up a hand. "Maybe she couldn't get either of them. Maybe Ray denied that he'd overheard anything and claimed that he's been buying Ullman stock purely on instinct. I just don't know, but I couldn't sit back and do nothing forever."

Donovan sat staring at her like the man of stone Brenda had accused him of being. "What do you want from me?"

"I don't know. I . . . just wanted you to know the truth."

"You and I seem to have different perceptions of the truth," he countered, and she knew he was thinking of the things she'd said to him when last they'd seen each other.

She averted her gaze, unable to face him. "I'm sorry," she whispered. "I shouldn't have said those things. I was angry and . . . and I didn't know what else to do."

"You were terrified. But then, you've been terrified of me ever since we met. The only difference is that now you've got due cause."

That there was terror now, she couldn't deny. It showed in the rigidity of her body, in her face, in her eyes as they shot to his. "You wouldn't . . . prosecute . . . would you?"

"It is illegal, what you did."

"But I didn't mean to do it. I didn't do it with ill intent. It was a mistake, and I've said I'm sorry, and if Ray can be convinced to get rid of his stock before the merger is made public and he makes any profit . . ."

"The fact remains that the SEC may already be on to you both."

She caught her breath. "Is it?"

He gave a negligent shrug. "I don't really know. I got my initial information from the people in New Orleans. To my knowledge, they haven't gone to the authorities. . .yet."

She sat farther forward. "Stop them, Donovan! You can, if you want. Explain that it was a mistake and that it's going to be corrected before anything comes of it."

"But I don't know that. You said it yourself. You don't know what Obermeyer's response is. And forgetting even that, why should I help you?" He was pressuring her as he never had before, and while it tore him apart to do so, he sensed he needed to do it for her sake, for *their* sake.

She looked around vainly for an answer. "Because . . . because we were friends once . . . and if you knew me at all you'd understand how badly I feel."

He took his time in responding, pensively rubbing his upper lip before dropping his hand. "How badly *do* you feel?"

"I feel awful! I'd never have come here today if that hadn't been so! After the things I said to you, you've got every right to kick me out. I'm ashamed of *everything*. You do know that, don't you, Donovan?"

He raised one brow, then lowered it. "I know that you don't think terribly highly of me as a person. You made that clear—"

"I was frightened! All right, that's what you want to hear, isn't it? I was frightened and I lashed out."

"And now you claim you didn't mean a word? Now that you need my help, you're apologizing? You've had a good long time to apologize, Liz. Why only now? Damn it, put that purse down! You'll ruin the leather if you keep strangling it that way." He heard his own harshness and knew that it was born of frustration. It killed him to be causing her pain, but he had to!

As though it were a hot potato, she dropped the purse to the floor and clutched her hands in her lap. "I couldn't face you before. I...I was afraid that you'd take my apology as a sign that I . . . that I . . ."

"Want me? I know you do, well, on one level at least. But that's where the terror comes in, doesn't it? You'll go to your grave a virgin because you're scared of making love."

Her voice was a mere breath. "It's not that."

"Then what is it?"

She simply shrugged and kept her chin low, her eyes downcast.

"But now you want my help." He leaned farther back in his chair and laced his fingers together over his middle. "Okay, Liz. I'll help you." She looked up at him, only to have the hope in her eyes fade when he went on. "But on one condition."

"What's . . . that?"

He hesitated for only an instant. She'd made her move; now he had to counter it. He didn't like what he was about to say, but he had to force a showdown. He had to free her of the shadow that dogged her, even if it meant coming across like a bastard. "That you move in with me. That you become my lover."

The blood rushed from her head and she felt dizzy. She clutched the arms of the chair but found little support. "You can't be serious."

"I am. Very much so. I know that you prize your freedom, that you like to make your own choices. Well, the choices are these. You can come to me of your own free will, or I'll go to the authorities. It's as simple as that." It wasn't really, because he'd never be able to turn her in. He was bluffing as never before. But hadn't he been the one to say that to win one had to operate in the most efficient manner possible?

She was shaking her head very slowly, trying to deny the fleeting images that crossed her mind, but tears began to gather at her lower lids and she sensed she was cornered. "Why are you doing this?" she whispered brokenly.

"Because I want you. I always have. I'd pretty much given up on you after last time, but since you've walked in here and put the tool right in my hands—"

"The weapon, you mean."

Determinedly he held his gaze steady. "Whatever. I still feel the same about you, and I've got you where I want you. You know, you were wrong about my being arrogant and cruel. The problem was that I was too *nice* where you were concerned. I should have been more forceful from the start. Then there wouldn't have been all this prancing around on tiptoes. My strategy was all wrong."

"A game. That's all it is. But I'm a nobody. You could play games with anyone else."

"I'm not looking to play games with anyone else."

"You want to make an example of me."

"No. This is private, between you and me. The rest of the world doesn't have to know a thing."

"You're having fun."

"I hope to. For that matter, I hope you will, too."

"You are cruel."

"Come on," he grumbled wearily. "We don't need more name-calling. That's what got you into trouble before."

"I bruised your ego then. You're taking revenge for what I said."

He didn't refute her charge. To do so would have been to tip his hand, and he felt shaky enough inside as it was.

"Donovan . . . please? Don't ask this of me."

He forced his mind away from the pain he was inflicting. It was for her own good, he told himself. *It had to work!* "You could refuse my offer, in which case the legal system will take over. You might not like that. I mean, white-collar crime or no, there's still the booking process and bail and a trial. And if you were to be convicted, you might be able to get away with a stiff fine, but I'm not sure you've got that kind of money. Chances are you'd spend a little time in jail. I doubt the judge would be too hard on you, though."

Liz stumbled from her chair and made for the door, but her knees were wobbling so badly that she could only clutch its knob and press her forehead to the wood.

"What's the matter, Liz? Finally putting terror in perspective?"

"My job . . . my future . . . it'd all be gone . . ."

"It's either that or your virginity. Seems to me the choice is pretty clear-cut. Of course, it's your choice. Your free choice. That's what you've always wanted, isn't it?"

"You really hate me, don't you?" she breathed.

She heard movement from her desk and when next he spoke it was from directly behind her. "Hate you? No." He put a light hand on her shoulder, then ran it over her back. Fortunately she couldn't see the agony in his eyes. "I just want to see this trembling put to better use. You'll tremble when I make love to you, Liz. You'll tremble and cry out and wonder what it was you ever fought." His voice grew soft in the way she'd known so well, "Because you'll feel like a million with me inside you, and so will I. Does that sound like hate to you?"

She was breathing hard, trying desperately not to cry. "I swore this . . . would never happen to me again. I swore I wouldn't let . . . anyone do this . . ."

He leaned into her, but she was beyond appreciating the support or the fact that his tone was more gentle and that he seemed to be talking as much to himself as to her. "Sometimes choices aren't much fun. Sometimes it's a matter of opting for the lesser of two evils. I wouldn't have had it this way, either, but things didn't quite work out the way I'd hoped."

She pressed pale fingers to the door. "How long . . ." Her voice was garbled, so she cleared her throat. "How long would this . . . arrangement last?"

"At least until the Ullman merger is formalized and made public. I'd want you under my thumb until then. As for the future, well, who's to say. You might find that you'll like what you've got."

"Please . . . don't make me . . ."

"I'm not making you do anything. You've got a choice."

"But . . . I can't . . ."

He straightened to his full height then. "Today's Thursday. You've got until Sunday noon to make your decision." He returned to his desk, and Liz turned her head to see him jotting on a small pad. He tore the top sheet off, then approached her. "My Manhattan address. I don't think you've ever been to my place here." She stared at the piece of paper. "Take it, Liz." When she still didn't move, he ducked away to retrieve her purse from the floor. He opened it, stuck the paper inside, then held it out. "Noon Sunday. If I haven't heard from you by then, I'll put in a call to a friend who happens to be on the SEC. He'll take it from there."

Quivering, Liz took the bag and paused only to blot her wet cheeks before passing through the door he'd opened. How she found her way out of the building she didn't know, or for that matter, how she managed to find her way home. She felt ill and more than once paused to lean against the side of a building, praying only that she wouldn't disgrace herself by being sick all over the pavement. She was marginally aware that more than one person stared at her, but she was beyond caring. The only thing that seemed to matter was reaching the familiar confines of her apartment, climbing into bed and pulling the covers over her head.

It was late in the afternoon when the phone rang. She listened to its peal, debating whether to answer it until she realized that Donovan might be calling with a reprieve. Scrambling free of the blankets, she grabbed up the receiver, only to find that it was her secretary, concerned when she hadn't returned. Not only had she missed a meeting, Cheryl Obermeyer had also been trying to reach her.

Liz explained that she wasn't feeling well and asked that any appointments she had scheduled for Friday be canceled. After pressing the button, Liz phoned Cheryl.

"He's a bastard, Liz. What else can I say. I've been working on him, our lawyer's been working on him, but he won't budge from his claim that he never heard a word from you. I mean, the guy may be my brother, but you know as well as I do that he's got no instinct for business, much less the stock market. He expects me to believe that his buying that Ullman stock is a shot in the dark. Who's he kidding? He's a waste! He refuses to believe that he's in legal trouble, and by the time he does it'll be too late."

Liz let out a long breath and fell back to the pillow. Ray's getting rid of the stock had been her only hope, and even then it had been a long shot that Donovan would have dropped things there. "It's okay, Cheryl. He'll be all right."

"How can he be all right? He's breaking the law. You know as well as I do that his buying that stock was no fluke."

"But he won't be prosecuted. I've...taken care of it."

"You've what? But how?"

"I talked with Donovan today. He won't report it. No one will ever know that it was anything but sheer luck that Ray chose this particular time to invest in Ullman."

"Are you sure? But even then, we'll know. I feel tainted simply by being related to Ray. You sound awful, Liz. You're not at the office, are you? I've been trying you there."

"I'm home."

"Are you sick?"

"I . . . I must have the flu or something. I'll be okay."

"Is there anything I can do? God, you've been wonderful about all this. It's a miracle you haven't washed your hands of us already, what with all we've put you through."

"It was my own fault, Cheryl. I was the one who let it slip."

"I asked Ray what he intended to do with the money he makes, and he informed me that he has designs on his own company. You know, Liz, I hope to God he does, because if he doesn't come to his senses and divest himself of that stock soon, hell will freeze over before I give him a thing. Dad's got limited time, and then the company will be mine, and there's *no way* I'll let him touch it!"

"Take it easy, Cheryl. He's your brother. He's immature and he's frustrated and—"

"He's stupid!"

"Well, there's no point in our rehashing that. Listen, I really do feel pretty lousy. I'm going to try to sleep. Can I talk with you another time?"

"Sure, Liz. *Is* there anything I can do?"

"No. But thanks anyway, Cheryl. And thanks for trying to talk with Ray. It's not your fault that he is the way he is."

"Mmm. I sometimes wonder about that. But . . . enough said for now. You take care of yourself. Will you let me know if you need anything?"

"I will. Bye, Cheryl."

LIZ HAD KNOWN what her choice had to be even before she'd left Donovan's office, yet through the next two days she agonized. She could barely eat, and what little sleep she got was inevitably interrupted by a nightmare that seemed to continue even after she'd woken.

She pictured herself being charged with the misuse of inside information, with conspiracy, with stock fraud or theft or embezzlement or whatever the official words were. She pictured herself going through the legal processes Donovan had described and remembered so recently having thought about many of the same things with regard to Jamie. The irony of it was too much. Too much.

She considered the possibility that Donovan was bluffing and thought of calling him on it. But the penalties were too harsh. Even aside from the legal ramifications, her job, her reputation in the field, her

security would all be gone. And without a job she
wouldn't be able to help Jamie. While one part of her
said that it would be good for him to have to stand on
his own two feet for once, the other, larger part couldn't
bear the thought of letting him down this way. She'd let
him down many times when they were children. She
just couldn't do it again.

So she accustomed herself to the only option that remained. She would go to Donovan's apartment at noon
on Sunday and submit to whatever he wished to do.
She tried to steel herself against the humiliation, the
mental pain she knew she'd have to endure, but she only
ended up more and more anguished. She felt so much
for Donovan . . . yet he'd see her and taunt her and, in
the end, find that the game wasn't half as much fun as
he'd anticipated.

Anticipation. What might be for him the best part
was for her the worst. As the hours passed she came to
realize this, and it was her sole saving grace. The pain,
the torment she was suffering now *had* to be worse than
the actuality.

She also realized something else. Perhaps it was by
way of rationalization, but a tiny part of her did want
to be Donovan's lover. She was stunned by the knowledge, but then, Donovan had been stunning her for
weeks, awakening feelings in her she'd thought herself
immune to. He aroused her physically. She knew all too
well how wonderful she felt in his arms. So what if he'd
send her home later? He was the one who was forcing
her into it. He was giving her the excuse to taste heaven,
if only once in her life. When Donovan was done with
her, her job, her future would still be intact. She'd sim-

ply have to pick up the pieces of her personal life and put them together again.

Sunday morning found her utterly calm. Numbness did that to a person, she knew, and she was grateful. She cleaned the apartment and put in a wash, then showered and put on a pair of slacks and a sweater. Taking a suit bag with her clothes for work and a small overnight bag for the few personal essentials she'd need, she left her apartment and started the walk to Donovan's.

It wasn't far, but the air was cold, as by rights December should be. And the spiritual warmth of the Christmas decorations in store windows eluded her as she walked on, barely seeing, intent only on reaching her destination.

8

At 11:55 Liz reached the address Donovan had scrawled on the small piece of paper. It was an elegant high rise in the East Eighties, with large glass doors in shining brass frames. Her hand was steady as she let herself in, her voice quiet when she gave the attendant her name. She watched him press a button on his phone, then announce her arrival, then nod at the response he received.

"Fifteenth floor, Ms Jerome," he said as he replaced the phone. "Mr. Grant's door is the second on the right."

"Thank you."

Had she been capable of feeling at that moment, she would have been proud of the way she walked toward the waiting elevator and stepped inside. She would have been proud of the way she walked out on the fifteenth floor, turned to the right and approached the second door. She looked composed and sure, and that composure barely faltered when Donovan opened the door.

His expression was shuttered as he raised his hand to look at his watch. "You're right on time. It's just noon." Then he surveyed her and her bags. "Is this all you've brought?"

"Yes," she answered quietly.

"Not very much for a prolonged stay."

"It may not be prolonged. After tonight the game will be done. You'll be glad to see me go."

"That wasn't our arrangement," he gently reminded her as he took the suit bag and overnight case from her hands. "You can pick up the rest tomorrow. Come on in and take off your coat. I've got brunch nearly ready."

Holding herself straight, she stepped inside. She blotted the sound of the closing door from her mind, much as she'd blotted out everything else all morning. "I'm not very hungry."

After setting her things down on a chair by the door, he helped her off with her coat, studying her closely all the while. She might have seen his concern if she'd been looking for it, but she wasn't. "You look like hell, Liz. Are you sick?"

"It's my usual pallor."

"Are you sick?"

"I . . . I haven't been able to sleep. That's all."

"Or eat. When was the last square meal you had?"

"I don't know."

"Then I'm glad I cooked."

"You were that sure I'd come?"

Without answering her he lifted the suit bag and overnight case again, headed down the hall and disappeared from view. She was still by the door when he returned. "You don't have to stand there, Liz. You can come in and sit down."

"I'm not sure what I'm supposed to be doing."

"For now you're supposed to be making yourself at home here, since this will be home for a while."

"You'll . . . we'll be staying here then?"

"Until the weekend. Then we'll go up to the house."

She nodded and walked forward, about to descend the two steps into the living room when Donovan stopped her. "Why don't you come into the kitchen with me. I've got to put everything out."

As though she'd only been waiting for his command, she turned and followed him. She watched from the door of the kitchen as he donned mitts and bent to take a large glass pan from the oven.

"What made you decide to come?" He set the pan on the stove top and reached toward the refrigerator, carefully hiding his relief that she'd showed, and his pleasure. He hesitated to soften outwardly, fearing that she might then plead for a reprieve, fearing that he might give in. But he had to go through with what he'd started.

"I didn't have much of a choice."

"You did have a choice." He'd taken out a container of orange juice and a bottle of wine.

"Then it was, as you put it yourself, a matter of choosing between the lesser of two evils."

He turned to lean back against the counter, facing her. "The other was that bad?"

"Yes."

"Did you hear from your friend?"

"Her brother's denying it."

Donovan shook his head in dismay, then shrugged. "You know, even if it all came to a trial, you'd probably get off with probation. You could argue that you were innocent of malicious intent. The judge might believe you."

"Then again, he might not. I can't take that chance." She'd thought it all out before, looking into any and every possibility, but she'd seen no escape. "My career is at stake. It would be damaged by the simple fact of the accusation being made, regardless of the outcome."

"Your career means that much to you?"

"Yes."

"Why?"

"It's just about the only source of self-respect I have. And I need the money to help Jamie out with his therapist."

Donovan considered that for a minute. Then he turned around, took two tall glasses from a cupboard and filled them with a mixture of orange juice and wine. Champagne, actually, Liz realized when he explained what he'd made.

"Mimosas. And a blintz soufflé. And fresh fruit." He sent her a pensive glance. "I think I'll heat muffins, too. You could use some fattening up."

Liz said nothing, but stood with her hands balled in the pockets of her slacks.

"Well, what do you think of my place?"

"I don't know. I haven't looked around."

"Then look. Start with this room. You liked my country kitchen. This is its city cousin."

Dutifully she ran her eye around the room. "Very nice."

His grin was weak. "Such enthusiasm. Close your eyes." When she looked puzzled, he repeated himself. "Close your eyes." She did. "Now tell me what you saw."

She hesitated for as long as she dared. "I . . . can't."

"That's what I thought." He sighed. "Well, you'll know later. Liz . . . open your eyes. Damn it, you're not a machine, y'know. I've got no intention of leading you through life here as though you didn't have a brain in your head."

"I'm sorry. You can always send me home."

"Oh-ho, no. The deal was that we'd be lovers, and that's exactly what we're going to be." He was purposely goading her to get a response, and if it hurt him to do it, he told himself it was necessary. "If you want to stand around here like a mummy, that's fine. But you're not going to weasel out of this by acting like an idiot."

Liz felt an inkling of anger, the first stirring of emotion she'd experienced in hours. "I'm not acting like an idiot. You've put me in a situation that's totally foreign to me. It's awkward, and I feel strange. What would you have me do—waltz in here all smiles when I'd rather be anywhere else?"

"Unnh!" He held up a finger. "The deal was that you'd come to me of your own free will."

"Words. Only words."

"And they'll be only words I pass to my SEC friend if I sense any more antagonism. You had your shot at me that day in your apartment. I've got enough ugliness to remember, without having more. Understood?"

Imprisoned by the determination in his gaze, she nodded once, then swallowed.

"Sit down," he murmured. "I'll just put the muffins in and then we'll eat."

Liz sat down at the small round table and stared at her place setting until the empty plate was removed and replaced by one filled to the brim with the goodies Donovan had prepared.

"I don't think I can eat all this," she said quietly."

"You can try. That's all I ask."

Lifting her fork, she began to pick at the soufflé.

"Why don't you take a drink. It'll loosen you up."

"I don't need loosening."

"You're tight as wire. Drink it, Liz. Then you'll *have* to eat, unless you want the champagne to go to your head, in which case you're apt to do something foolish."

"That's how this all happened. If only I hadn't had that second drink . . ."

"It's water over the dam. You've got to move on." That play was long since done, though it had been instrumental in setting up the one they were working through now. He took a drink, then a forkful of the soufflé. "Mmm. Not bad. You weren't at work yesterday."

She eyed him. "You checked up on me?"

"No. But I did see Brenda, and your name came up. She said you were sick. Were you that disturbed after our talk Thursday?"

"Yes."

"But you seem cool as a cuke now."

"You gave me two choices. I picked one."

"And you've accepted your fate."

"Only because I have to. That doesn't mean I have to like it." She wasn't being wholly truthful, she knew. But that small part of her that tingled at the thought of

Donovan making love to her was being overpowered by nervousness, which in turn was tempered by the numbness she'd set protectively about herself.

"Careful, Liz. I can still make the call . . . For God's sake, eat!"

Liz ate, thought it might have been cardboard that agonizingly worked its way down her throat and into her stomach. The drink did little to loosen her up. And Donovan remained silent until they were done.

"Coffee?" he asked as he carried their dishes to the sink.

"No, thank you."

"Then I'll clean up here. Why don't you wander around. I'll be done in a minute and we can take a walk."

Liz went into the living room and sat in a chair until Donovan joined her.

"Will you be warm enough?" he asked as he held her coat for her. "You don't have a hat or anything, and it's pretty cold out."

"I'll be fine." She buttoned the coat up to her neck and buried her hands in her pockets, but Donovan insistently retrieved one and closed his fingers around it.

They took the elevator down and left the building, heading toward Fifth Avenue.

"At least you've got comfortable shoes on," he commented, eyeing her soft leather flats. "You'll have to bring boots over, though. We're apt to get snow any day, and there's nothing more fun, especially upstate, than going out for walks in the snow."

"I've got heels in my bag for work tomorrow," was all she said.

By the time they'd walked several blocks Liz was shivering. She freed her hand to turn up the collar of her coat, but Donovan quickly snatched it back and tucked it, along with his own, into the pocket of his heavy jacket.

"If you're too cold, we can turn back." He had so many second thoughts about what he was forcing, but this was the only one he could express.

"I'm fine. The cold feels good."

"Numbing? Is that what you want?"

"It helps."

He tipped up his chin and smiled. "Y'know, tomorrow you'll be laughing at all this. You don't want to be numb, Liz. You want to enjoy yourself."

"I want to be numb."

"Don't have much faith in my ability as a lover?"

"It's not your ability I'm worried about."

"Then yours? Hell, Liz, you'll be terrific. I've never been worried about that. I mean, it'll be new at first, maybe a little painful, but if you trust me and let yourself go, you'll get over that and it'll be great."

Liz felt her cheeks flare beneath their chill, but she simply stared ahead. Donovan looked at her from time to time, but she refused to return his gaze. So they walked, briskly and in silence. As they approached the Plaza, the sidewalk traffic picked up and she was forced closer to him. Each time their hips brushed she stiffened; each time he ordered her to relax. But relaxation was beyond her. The only thing she could do was concentrate on keeping one foot moving after the other.

Rockefeller Center was seasonally cheerful, with Christmas lights in abundance and a huge tree surveying all. Donovan edged to the front of the gathered crowd so that he and Liz could look down at the skaters on the rink for a time. Then they headed for a coffee shop on Sixth Avenue, where he ordered hot chocolates for them both.

"I'll pick you up from work tomorrow and we can go back to your apartment for more clothes. There's a party on Thursday night we'll be going to, and—"

"You don't need me along. I thought you said that this wasn't going to be a public spectacle."

"It's not going to be a public spectacle. What happens in the privacy of our bedroom is between you and me. As far as anyone else is concerned, Thursday night you're my date. You're right. I don't *need* you along. But I *want* you along, which is why you'll be coming."

"Why would you want me along, other than to make a spectacle of me?"

In a moment's exasperation Donovan scowled at her. Then, regaining control, he softened. "I want you with me because I enjoy your company—"

"Even now? I can't believe it."

He grinned. "Right now, you're a real challenge. You've convinced yourself that you don't feel a thing, like a martyr being led to the stake, and it's rather fun trying to poke holes in that bravado. But don't forget, I've seen you differently. Which is why I say that I enjoy your company. You're intelligent and thoughtful." He tipped his head as he stared at her, into her. "There's something about you, a warmth, a compassion, that appeals to people—at least, it did to me from the first. And besides—" he smiled his thanks at the waitress who delivered their drinks and left "—by Thursday night you'll be feeling very good."

"Thanks to you?"

"Thanks to *you*. Liz, you don't seem to realize that you're your own worst enemy. You've got yourself convinced that you're ugly and unappealing, that there's no credible reason I should be attracted to you. But you're wrong. And you're going to find that out for yourself before long." He paused to sip from the steaming cup before him and motioned for her to do the same.

"It's too hot."

"Then blow on it. At least hold the cup. It'll warm your hands."

She did hold the cup, though it did little to warm her, so she set it down, at which point Donovan took her hands between his and chafed them. "Before, you said that your job was your only source of self-respect. That's what I don't understand. You've got a hell of a lot to be proud of besides your job. You've got character and presence, and I'm sure that legion of friends you've got could say a whole lot more."

She shrugged and put her hands back around her hot chocolate.

"No comment?" he prodded.

"No."

"Why not? You're usually right on the stick telling me off when I give you compliments."

"It's not worth the effort." She lifted the cup and sipped from it, staring straight ahead.

"But you're depriving me of fun if you don't argue."

"That's the point."

"Then you're seething inside, but biting your tongue."

"I'm not seething."

"It'd give me too much satisfaction, right?"

"Something like that." Actually, she realized that she was testing him. She wondered how much he'd take before disillusionment set in.

He laughed. "You are a gem, Liz. And speaking of gems, how are your ears? I see you're still wearing the earrings. I'd have thought you'd have ripped them out after Thursday."

Lowering her gaze, she admitted softly, "I can't."

"What do you mean, you can't?"

"I'm afraid to take them out. I have a squeamish stomach. I told you I'm not good at dealing with pain."

"But you've had to do ... something with them, haven't you?"

"I put alcohol on them twice a day and twist them. The doctor told me not to take them out for a couple of weeks."

"And it's been a couple of weeks. Weren't you planning to change them at some point?"

"I ... suppose."

"But—" he held up a finger "—you don't have any others. *That's* what we can do one other night this week. We can go shopping for earrings."

"I'm not spending good money on jewelry."

"Fine. I will."

She looked at him sharply. "You will not. I may be forced to share your bed, but I'm *not* going to be paid for it."

He grinned and punched the air with his fist. "Atta girl. Fight with me. Tell me where to get off."

She glared, then carefully schooled her expression to one of blandness and looked away. Donovan was undaunted.

"Then it's settled. Mmm, I think pearls would be nice. Very simple. Very elegant. And don't worry, love. I'll help you put them in. I've got a strong stomach, so you can pass out or throw up or do whatever your little heart desires, but when you come to, your ears will look super."

"It was dumb," she muttered. "I never should have had them pierced."

"Don't be silly. Now that it's done, I can buy you really *expensive* earrings without having to worry about their falling off."

Realizing she was being goaded to once again speak out against being "kept," Liz ignored him and took another drink. When she set the cup down, Donovan lifted her coat from the back of the chair.

"Shall we go?"

She hesitated for an instant, almost regretting leaving the coffee shop, which was so clearly, if relatively, safe ground. Then she caught herself. She wanted this over. She wanted Donovan to do what he would and then let her go home.

Without a word she slipped her arms into her coat, stood and buttoned it. As he had before, Donovan tucked her hand into his pocket, and they started back the way they'd come. This time, though, Liz had trouble keeping up, so Donovan slowed the pace.

"Got cold feet?" he teased, leaning close to her ear.

"They've been cold for three days."

"I'll have to warm them up for you when we get home."

"They'll be fine."

"Maybe you'd like a hot bath. That'd warm you up."

"I had a hot shower this morning and it didn't help."

"Getting ready for me, were you?"

She gave him a quelling stare but said nothing more.

By the time they reached his building, Liz understood why Donovan had walked her so far. She was exhausted, and she cursed the fact, because she needed every bit of her strength to remain composed through what she was sure lay ahead.

Once inside his condominium, she braced herself as best she could. Donovan removed his coat and took hers, hanging them both in the closet by the door. Then he took her hand and she stumbled after him down the hall, fully expecting to find herself in his bedroom, with the awesome moment at hand. To her amazement he drew her into a room opposite the other door.

"I want to catch the end of the Knicks' game. Okay?"

She nodded dumbly, then found herself being led to a long leather couch. After depositing her in its richly scented folds, he crossed to a television set, turned it on, switched the channel, then returned. The game was in its third quarter, with the Knicks trailing. Donovan grunted when the opposing team scored another basket, then he spoke to Liz without taking his eyes from the screen.

"Do you like basketball?"

"Not particularly."

"That's probably because you've never watched enough of it to get involved in the game. Oooooh!" A Bernard King lay-up whirled around the rim of the basket before falling off, but King made the rebound himself and promptly dunked the ball. "Heeey! Good goin', Bernard!"

"I'm sure he can hear you."

Donovan ignored her dry comment. "The Knicks are a super team this year. Something seems to have jelled. 'Course, the same's true of both the Celtics and the Sixers. Their records are better, though Bernard, God bless him, is the top scorer in the league. Whoa. Did you see that? A three-pointer! Atta way, Knicks!"

Liz looked away from the screen. She focused first on the stereo set, then the nearby bookshelves, then an oil painting that hung on one wall. It was an abstract.

"No, not a time out now, you dummy!" Donovan screamed at the opposite coach, then directed quieter words at Liz. "Do you like it?"

"Like what?"

"The painting."

"It's bizarre," she mumbled.

Donovan grinned in intentional misinterpretation. "I think so, too. It's challenging, somehow. I can sit here for hours staring at it, trying to decide what I see, but what I see always seems to reflect my mood. What do you see?"

"A blinding nightmare."

"I see excitement . . . discovery. The artist is a friend of mine. From the old days, actually. He's a little bizarre himself, but I love him. There we go. All tied up."

He lowered his voice in urging. "Come on, Knicks, come on."

Suddenly feeling the need to move, Liz jumped from the sofa and walked to the bookshelves. She stared at their contents for a minute, then walked to the window. Minutes later she was prowling the room.

"Sit down and relax, Liz."

"I *can't* relax."

"The waiting's finally getting to you, is it?"

He'd hit the nail on the head. "I don't like basketball, and there's nothing else for me to do."

"I could give you some crayons and a piece of paper and you could draw me a picture."

"I'm not a child."

"So you're not," he said, slowly twisting to face her. Having made a complete circle of the room, she was back where she'd begun by the bookshelves. "I'd say you're impatient. Maybe excited?"

Liz had had it. Her outward calm fled, along with the numbness that had protected her earlier. Excited? Oh, yes. But she was also terrified, and that made her perverse. "Don't flatter yourself, Donovan," she gritted. "It's occurring to me, more and more each minute, that I wasn't so wrong in what I said to you that day. You *are* arrogant. *And* bullheaded. *And* narrow-minded. And some day that cockiness of yours is going to get you into a whole load of trouble."

As she railed on, the easy indulgence that had dominated Donovan's expression for much of the afternoon fled. In its place was a certain grimness. "I told you to be careful, Liz," he warned. "You're skating on thin ice."

She threw up her hands. "I don't care! Falling in and drowning would be better than what I'm going through now. You're playing with me, just like you've always played with me. Well, I'm not a toy! And I'm not made of steel!"

He looked at her for a minute, then finally spoke in a tone of deadly calm. "Is that the way you feel?"

"That's *precisely* the way I feel."

"Are you sure?"

"Of course, I'm sure!"

He thought a moment longer, then sat deeper into the sofa and spread his arms to either side atop the back cushions. Though he looked confident and relaxed, inside he was a bundle of nerves. "Okay," he said quietly. "Take off your clothes."

Liz stood perfectly still. She couldn't believe what he'd said. "Ex-excuse me?"

"I said, take off your clothes."

She took a step back, but came up against the bookshelves. "Uh, look, it's okay. I'll just, uh, I'll just watch your game—" But he was shaking his head in a determined manner. "Hey, Donovan, I'm really sorry. It's just that I'm nervous and I'm not really in control—"

"Take them off now," he said softly, "or I'll make that call."

"This isn't like you," she said, gulping. "It's out of character. You were always so understanding."

He didn't want to feel understanding now. He was pushing himself as desperately as he was pushing her. "It's what you've done to me."

She stared at him, but there was no yielding in his face, no compassion in his tone. Very slowly he lowered one hand toward the phone, which sat on the end table.

"Please, Donovan," she whispered, her eyes wide, "don't do this to me." The tiny part of her that had wanted his lovemaking was stunned into neutrality. She hadn't dreamed he'd approach it this way!

"You can start with the sweater."

"I . . . but it's . . . broad daylight."

"So much the better. Go on. The sweater."

Her breath was coming in short gasps. "I can't . . . don't make me . . ."

"You can and you will. I'll give you ten seconds to start. Ten, nine, eight, seven . . ."

Hands trembling, Liz reached for the hem of her sweater and drew it up. It was over her head and on the floor before she looked at him again. The pleading in her eyes went unheeded.

"Now the blouse."

"Donovan . . . I'm begging you . . ."

His fingers brushed the telephone. "The blouse, Liz."

The threat of that gesture, coupled with that in his gaze, made her swallow hard. Tucking her chin low, she began to release the buttons of her blouse. When she was done, she clutched the center tabs together.

"Off, Liz."

She glanced toward the television. "In front of . . . of them?"

He made a gutteral sound before bounding from the sofa and turning off the set. "They wouldn't see a thing, but if it makes you feel better . . ." He resumed the pose of the relaxed spectator, though his insides were in knots. His hand dangled ever closer to the phone. "Six, five . . ."

She struggled out of the blouse and dropped it, then stood with her shoulders hunched forward and her eyes downcast.

"Go on, Liz. You know what to do."

"No!" she whispered.

"You won't do it?" He lifted the receiver, dropping it only when she reached for the snap of her jeans. He watched her bend over, pushing the jeans down her legs, stepping out of her flats to push the denim from her feet.

She didn't straighten all the way. She couldn't. Even if her stomach hadn't been cramped, the humiliation she felt would have prevented it.

"Take off the tights."

"Please . . ." she begged.

"Do it!" He was furious at her for making him drag it on this way.

She peeled the navy tights from her hips and legs and had to struggle to keep her balance as she pulled them from her feet. Her legs were shaking, as were her hands. She wrapped her arms around her waist, feeling chilled inside and out.

"You're almost there, Liz. Now the bra."

Frantically she tried to think of some way to escape the hell she was in, but she was trapped. She could refuse outright, but the consequences . . . It took her a minute to release the back catch because her fingers seemed boneless, but finally she added that piece of nylon to the pile by her feet. Instinctively she shielded herself with her hands, but he wouldn't have it.

"Put your arms down. I want to see you."

Only with a determined effort did she do as he'd ordered. Donovan said nothing for a minute. She felt tears well in her eyes, then trickle down her cheeks, but she kept her head bent, unable to look at him.

"Okay," he said more quietly. "Now take off your panties."

She hunched her shoulders even more, doing the only thing she could to protect herself from his gaze. If only they were in the bedroom and it was dark...but...like this?

"Liz . . ." he warned.

Crying quietly, she slipped her cold hands inside the elastic band at her waist and pushed the panties off. Then she stood before him totally naked, trembling as she endured one nightmare and relived another.

"He...he made me...do this, too," she sobbed softly, unable to stem the words because embarrassment, humiliation, defeat had robbed her of what little pride she might have had. She was shaking uncontrollably. "He made me . . . stand . . . in front of him . . . and take my clothes . . . off . . . just like this...and then—"

"What?" Donovan cut in in a whisper, suddenly before her, his hands on her cold quaking shoulders.

She barely registered his presence. The words just seemed to spill. "My father . . . he told me how . . . how ashamed I should be . . . how disgraceful I was. That I shouldn't . . . shouldn't ever think that . . . that someone might want . . . me . . ." She broke down completely then, weeping copiously. But Donovan pulled her instantly against him, her face pressed to his chest, his trembling hands roaming her back as though he had to warm, to soothe, to protect every inch of her.

"Oh my God," he murmured brokenly, agonizingly, "oh my God . . . what have I done."

He hugged her to him and rocked her gently, then, keeping her upper body pressed close, he slipped an arm beneath her knees, lifted her and hurried from the den. She continued to cry, and he ran the last few steps to his bedroom, only releasing her legs to snatch his robe from the closet. As quickly as he could he slipped her arms into the sleeves and belted the lush terry fabric around her waist. Then, lifting her against him again, he sat down on the edge of the bed and held her tightly.

"I'm sorry, Elizabeth," he cried against her hair. "So sorry. I didn't know . . . I'd never have made you do that . . . if only you'd told me sooner . . . I knew that there had to be something, but you wouldn't tell me and I got so damned impatient with loving you and being blocked out."

She cried for a while longer, her body curled into a ball on his lap. Over and over he whispered soft words of apology and love, while he hugged her and rocked her. He felt her pain and suffered. He understood her humiliation and was filled with shame. He held her tighter, loving her with every ounce of his being. Then, when her sobs had finally begun to ease, he took her face in his hands and turned it to his.

"Look at me," he whispered. Her eyes were closed. He brushed damp tendrils of hair from her brow. "Please, sweetheart, look at me. I know you've got every right not to, but I need you to see me and hear me and know what I'm feeling."

She hiccuped softly and squeezed her eyes shut, pushing the last tears from her lids. He blotted them with his thumbs.

"Elizabeth . . .?"

She opened her eyes, looked at him, then away.

"Liz . . .?"

She met his gaze then, but with timidity.

"I don't want you to be frightened of me. I've never wanted that," he said, speaking very, very softly and gently. "I love you, Elizabeth. No, don't shake your head. It's the truth. I would have told you sooner but I was trying to go slow when you seemed threatened, and I didn't know what it was that was bothering you. I didn't think you'd believe me, and you don't, but that's okay because I'm going to spend the rest of my life proving it to you. Don't shut your eyes again, sweetheart. Please?" Only when she opened them did he go on.

"How old were you when your father did that to you?"

She bit her lip, but he prodded, still in that doe-soft tone. "How old were you?"

"Tw-twelve . . . and thirteen . . . and on . . ."

"Just when you were reaching adolescence. Just when you were developing as a woman." With a groan he pressed her head to his chest and held her that way until he'd regained his composure. "No wonder you're convinced that you're ugly and unappealing," he murmured, then held her back so he could look at her again. There was an intensity in his gaze this time. "Your father must be a very, very sick man. I wouldn't begin to try to explain why he did what he did. And it does no good rehashing the past. It's the present and the future I'm thinking about." Again he framed her face with his hands. "Elizabeth, you *are* beautiful. I know you don't believe it, but you *are*. I've seen your body, and there's *nothing wrong* with it. It's just as it should be." He cocked his head. "I mean, it's not like you've got a breast sticking out of your navel."

He was rewarded by a self-conscious laugh, which died as soon as it emerged but was a victory of sorts nonetheless.

"That's better." Smiling, he feather-brushed her lips with his thumbs. "Beauty is as beauty does. Have you ever heard that expression?" Very slowly, she nodded. "It applies to you as I've never known it to apply to anyone else. Especially now that I know what you've lived with all these years. You give so much to people, to friends, business associates. Look at what you do for Jamie."

When another thought intruded he frowned. "Liz, what did your father do to him?" When she simply stared at him unsurely, he coaxed. "Please. I want to know, to understand."

It took Liz a long time before she could answer, and then it was in a whisper. "He beat him."

Donovan closed his eyes for a moment. "Oh, God."

But Liz wasn't done. Her words spilled quickly, slurring together at times. "I used to stand in another room wanting to go to Jamie's defense, but I was too scared that Dad would turn on me instead so all I could do was to comfort Jamie afterward and hurt for him and always feel so guilty."

"Oh, God," Donovan murmured again, then grew suddenly fierce. "Did he ever touch you?" She shook her head quickly. "He never tried to molest you?"

"No. He only did what I told you . . . and more often it was just words . . . ugly words."

Donovan had to know there was nothing else. "I don't want you hiding anything from me. The time for that's over."

"No. That was all."

Donovan took a deep, slightly ragged breath. "That was enough." He propped her more comfortably in the crook of his shoulder. "You've never told anyone about this before, have you?" She shook her head. "And all this time you've gone through life believing that you'd repulse any man who looked at you . . . God, he should be beaten himself. To do that to his own daughter, when she's such a beautiful, beautiful person." He saw that she hadn't opened her mouth to argue, so he pressed on. "I do love you, Liz. I want you to know that. I do love you."

"But you'd given up on me. You were ready to turn me in to the police."

"I wouldn't have done that. It was an empty threat. I knew I had to bring this all to a head somehow. That seemed the only way. You were right. It was out of character. Donovan Grant, the laid-back, happy-go-lucky genius. Well," he sighed, "he's got feelings like the rest of us, and when he's in love, I'm afraid he's not quite so laid-back and happy-go-lucky. At least, not when he's dying inside because the woman he loves wants him out of her life."

"I never wanted that," she murmured. "I was just . . . just so afraid of letting it go further."

She felt a tension enter him, saw the vulnerability on his face. "I know this may be too much to ask after all I've done, but I've got to ask. I trust that you'll tell me the truth." He hesitated, never once taking his eyes from hers. "Do you, uh, could you love me, even just a little?"

He was the old Donovan then, baring himself, speaking sincerely and Liz felt her chill begin to fade. It was one thing for him to say that he loved her, another for him to ask—not tell, but ask—if she loved him back. But he'd trusted her to tell him the truth, and much as it hurt her, she couldn't lie.

"I don't know, Donovan," she said very softly. "I've pushed the idea of love from my mind for so long that I'm not sure I'm ready to believe in it. Maybe I do love you. Maybe that's why I was so threatened, because I wanted so badly to please you but knew I'd only disappoint you—"

"You *haven't* disappointed me, love. Nothing you've done has disappointed me, except maybe that day when you lashed out at me, and if that was because the seeds of love were there and you were torn and upset, I honestly can't blame you. Knowing what I do now, I can understand why you were so threatened. Not agree, mind you, because I love the way you look, but I do understand now why you don't believe in yourself." His smile was gentle enough to melt another layer of her chill. "That's what we're going to have to work on, you and me."

"Are you . . . going to keep me here?"

"By force, no. I only did it before out of desperation. But I won't do it again, Liz. No more threats. No more secrets. We've gone beyond those. When I think of a future without you it's pretty dismal, and if there's any chance that you could grow to love me . . . well, I can live with that." He grinned. "It's a challenge, really, getting you to love me back."

"What about . . ." Her eyes shifted briefly to the bed.

"I still want to make love to you. I don't think that'll ever change. But I want you to feel better about yourself first, and better about me." He paused. "I would like you to stay with me. There's so little other time, what with both of our jobs—though I want you to take over the DIG Group work again."

"You don't like Brenda? She's very good, and she's adorable."

"I want *you*. And I want every minute we spend together to be good." He hesitated once more. "Liz, if you stay here I won't push you. I mean, there's only this one bed, but it's plenty big and I'll put pillows between us if you want, but what I'd really like is to be able to hold you in the night. We don't have to make love. Only when you want it. But I've dreamed of waking up with you there, and . . . and . . . you have to take *some* pity on me . . ."

His lips were curving into a boyish grin that she simply couldn't resist. If she wanted to be truthful with herself, she'd never been able to resist it, though she'd tried, how she'd tried.

Her own grin was more tentative. "I will."

"You'll stay?"

She nodded, buoyed by his obvious pleasure.

He hugged her so tightly his arms trembled and she feared for a minute her ribs would crack. "O-kay!" he said with feeling, then set her back. "What say you get dressed, then we can go to your place and get more of your things and drop them back here, then go out to dinner somewhere special—I have just the place in mind—then—"

"Donovan?"

"Yes, love?"

"Could we make the dinner another time?"

His face fell. "This sounds familiar."

"No, it's not that," she was quick to reassure him. "After we get my things, could we just come back here and eat? I'm . . . I'm afraid I'll fall asleep if we have to sit out dinner at a fancy restaurant. It's been a . . . tiring week."

The relief in his expression was as good as a prize. "Sure, Liz. And you do look beat. But beautiful." He grinned, and on impulse swooped down and sealed her lips with a kiss. Then, nearly as quickly, he pulled back. "I'm sorry. Would you rather I not do that?"

The smile she gave him was the first honest-to-goodness one she'd manufactured in days. "I kind of liked it," she said shyly.

But rather than repeating the kiss, Donovan put his arms around her and hugged her.

Very slowly she slid her arms up and hugged him back.

9

DONOVAN LEFT LIZ in the bedroom while he retrieved her clothes, then waited in the living room, giving her the privacy she needed, until she'd dressed and joined him. They took a cab to her apartment, and an hour later, another back to his place with two suitcases in hand. He set some steaks on to broil while she neatly placed her things in the drawers and closets he'd cleared. By the time she'd followed her nose to the kitchen, she was starved.

"It's about time," was his reaction when she told him as much. "You really haven't eaten all week, have you?"

"Not much."

"Well," he declared, setting filled plates on the table, "you can make up for it now." He halted just before sitting to gently stroke her hair. "Feeling better?"

She smiled. "Much."

"I'm glad." He pressed a quick kiss to her head, then sat and began to eat. "I'll pick up a telephone-answering machine tomorrow, and we can set it up at your place after work. No one knows where you are, and if someone tries to reach you there'll be no problem. All you have to do is to leave my number on the recorder... better still, let me call the phone company first. They may be able to automatically forward your calls. That'd spare you having to make explanations."

She finished chewing a mouthful of steak and cut into her baked potato. Though hunger seemed her first priority, she was touched by his concern that she not be put in an awkward position. "And when a man answers 'my' number?"

"You can, uh, say it's your cleaning person."

She grinned. "I don't have a cleaning person."

"Then . . . the plumber?"

"I could just say that you're my boyfriend."

He grinned back. "I'd like that."

"'Course, most of my friends won't believe me and then I'll *really* have explaining to do. Maybe I'd better stick with the plumber."

Donovan could see she was teasing because her grin lingered. "You can tell anyone who's interested that it's your boyfriend and that anything more is none of their business. A little smugness wouldn't hurt. You haven't had much experience with that, have you?"

"Afraid not."

"Well, it's about time you begin. You've got a brilliant, successful, good-looking-as-hell guy in love with you. You have a right to be smug."

Blushing, Liz directed her gaze to her food.

"Liz?"

"Mmm?"

"What are you feeling? I mean, in many ways it's been an awful day for you, and I know you're exhausted, but I keep wondering whether you're happy . . . or frightened . . . or embarrassed . . . or excited."

She thought for a minute. "A little of each, I guess."

"Explain. Tell me."

Setting her fork down, she eyed him hesitantly. "You do have a beautiful place here, Donovan. I think the country house is still my favorite, but I can be very comfortable here."

"About *me*. Tell me what you're feeling about me."

It was harder to explain her feelings because their expression was all so new to her. But she tried, sensing Donovan's genuine need to know. "I'm feeling happy. You're right. You're brilliant and successful and good-looking as hell. In the minutes I let myself believe that you love me, I feel happy and excited, almost overwhelmingly so."

"But in the other minutes?"

Her eyes clouded. "I feel scared. Scared that it's all a fluke, too good to believe. Scared that you'll tire of me in a few days or a week or a month and that you'll see me for what I am."

"You are *not*—"

"For what I've always *seen* myself as being," she corrected. "I do still see myself that way, Donovan. It's habit, perhaps. Or reality," she said more softly, then raced on before he could argue. "And I also feel a little frightened. I've never lived with a man . . . well, not in that sense."

"I'll give you all the privacy you need, sweetheart. You've got space until you decide you don't need it as much."

"I know," she said quietly, lifting her fork, then holding it suspended above her steak. Once started, her thoughts flowed. "I'm also worried that my insecurities will haunt me whenever we're out somewhere and there are other women in the room." She pressed her lips together for a minute. "When I was talking with Cheryl at her party that night, she said that if I didn't want you, I should give you her number. I felt it then— jealousy, unsureness. And again when Brenda was talking about everything she was doing to make you see her as a woman."

"Brenda was doing that? I didn't notice a thing because I couldn't stop thinking of you. As for Cheryl, I've never met the woman. But—" he reached over and squeezed her hand "—believe me, I have met lots and lots of others, and not one of them has captivated me the way you have."

She chewed on her lip, then darted him a sidelong glance. "What if I don't please you in bed?"

"You will. I told you, I've never had doubts about that."

"But I don't know what to do."

"I'll show you. And because I'll have been able to do that, it'll be all that much better. If you want to look at it one way, I'll be to blame if things aren't right. After all, I'm supposed to be the experienced one. And I *know* the passion's there in you, Liz. I've had glimpses of it from time to time. Hey, don't get all flustered. That was a compliment. Do you remember when you first told me you were a virgin and I said that it was a gift?" He waited until she'd nodded. "Well, it is. I've been with women who are as experienced as the local madam, and I've spent my time with them wondering who taught them what they know and who'll be the one to teach them more. It's definitely taken something from the relationship, at least from my own feelings toward the relationship." He paused, thinking. "But I think it'd be different even if you weren't a virgin. *You're* different. And special. And when you look at me the way you are now, I feel like I'm the only man on earth. It's a nice feeling, Liz. Believe me, it's a very, very nice feeling." He smiled at her a minute longer, then gave her hand a parting pat. "Eat up. You warned me you might fall asleep, and that'd *really* bruise my ego."

"I said in a restaurant."

"Methinks here, too. You can only prop those lids up so long."

"It's all the wine I've drunk," she teased, making no effort to deny his claim.

He eyed the glasses, which were filled with nothing more potent than water. "Good thing I broke out the best," he said with a chuckle. "Lord only knows *what* would have happened with the cheap stuff."

Liz chuckled, too, then set to finishing every last bit of food on her plate. By then her head was all but wobbling on her neck, so Donovan suggested she go to bed. He walked her to the door of the kitchen, then turned her to him.

"Should I put pillows between us?"

"No."

"Will you be frightened if you wake up in the morning and find me holding you?"

"Maybe a little . . . at first."

"Just remember that I love you and that I won't do anything but hold you. It might be my own personal need to reassure myself that you're really here. Okay?"

She nodded, and he turned her and sent her off while he stayed in the kitchen. She was nervous taking her nightgown from the drawer and went into the bathroom to undress. But minutes after she'd carefully let herself into the far side of the bed she was asleep.

The next morning when she woke, Donovan was quietly holding her, and she found that she liked it very, very much.

MONDAY WENT BY IN A WHIRL for Liz, with no less than five of her associates commenting on how wonderful she looked. Well rested, they said, and full of color. She had a smile—yes, a smug one—for each of them.

Tuesday morning when she awoke, she was in Donovan's arms again. This time, she took stock of her surroundings, namely his chest, which was solid and covered by a soft furring of hair and fragrant in an utterly manly way beneath her cheek. She touched him, timidly skirting one nipple, then lifted her lips for his kiss when his quiet gasp told her he was awake.

"I like it when you touch me," he murmured against her mouth.

"It felt good. You're very warm."

"Mmm." He kissed her again, more thoroughly this time, then set her gently back. "We have to get up. You've got a nine-o'clock appointment. Want to take the bathroom first?"

She nodded and rolled to her side of the bed, tugging her nightgown down as she climbed out. She was halfway to the bathroom when Donovan called her back.

"Liz? One more kiss?"

Cheeks rosy, she returned to him, savoring his kiss until, with a light pat to her bottom, he sent her off.

By Wednesday morning her legs were entwined with his when she awoke. She felt comfortable and surprisingly secure, and grew more adventurous with the exploratory hand she ran over his chest and his arms. His tempered strength delighted her.

"Do you always wear pajama bottoms, or have you put them on for my benefit?" she asked after he'd given her a good-morning kiss.

"The latter, I'm afraid. I usually sleep in the buff."

She set her head down on his chest and dropped her gaze to his hips where his pajamas rode low. Then, without thinking of the consequences, she slid her palm down the dark, narrowing trail of hair to that point.

Donovan sucked in a sharp breath. "Oooh, sweetheart, you're playing with fire."

She snatched her hand away and quickly raised her head. "I'm sorry. I didn't think—"

"Shh." He pressed her head back down. "It's okay. It's just that I want you to touch me there, too. Just thinking of it does things to me."

The idea that she could so easily excite him was almost incredible, yet when she looked down his body she saw it was so. Her fingers itched, unsure but tempted. In the end it was curiosity that gave movement to her hand. It inched slowly past his waist, then his navel, then over the band of his pajamas until his tumescence was not mere vision but hard fact.

"That's it," he whispered hoarsely. He covered her hand with his and moved it gently up and down, up and down, until his breath was uneven, his entire body tense. "I, uh, I think that's enough." He swallowed loudly, then cleared his throat. "I'm a little short on control this time of day." He drew her hand up to cover his heart, which beat strong and fast against it.

What Liz hadn't expected was that the feel of his sex would touch off sensual reverberations in her own body, yet it did. A warmth spread from her breasts to her loins, and for the first time she knew true frustration. But Donovan was setting her gently back to her side of the bed.

"Can we meet at lunchtime? I thought we might go shopping."

"Shopping?"

"I'd like to buy you a dress for Thursday night."

"Donovan, you don't have to—"

"I know I don't have to, and I know you've got a perfectly beautiful dress hanging in the closet, and you've already told me your feelings about being 'kept.' But I *want* to buy you something. My motives are purely selfish. Will you deny me the pleasure?"

She rolled her eyes. "Talk about guilt trips. How can I refuse when you put it that way?" In truth, she was tickled pink, even more so when he beamed.

So he picked her up at the office and, hand in hand, they headed for the exclusive department store Donovan had in mind. He stayed with her until she'd selected—actually, he had to help with the selecting because he wanted the best, which she shied away from when she caught sight of the price tag—and tried on a stunning silk dress of a burgundy shade that brought out rather than overpowered her features. After settling the account with the salesperson, he excused himself, claiming he had one or two purchases of his own to make, and arranged to meet Liz by the front door in ten minutes.

When she arrived, he had a box under one arm and was looking vaguely sheepish. "Okay," she grinned. "What did you buy?"

"Oh, something . . . personal."

Envisioning briefs or an athletic support, or some other bit of intimate male attire, she blushed and asked no more. Grinning, he took the dress box from her arms and ushered her across the street to a jewelry store, where he insisted on buying her a pair of elegant pearl studs.

"Donovan, I can't let you—"

"Of course you can. They'll look smashing with the dress, even more smashing with your complexion. Besides, I haven't had this much fun since . . . since I shopped for you in San Francisco, and before that, well, I can't even remember."

One side of her lips turned down. "What if I can't put them on?"

"I told you I'd help. We can do it tonight, and you'll have plenty of time to recover before the party."

"I don't know. I'm starting to get really nervous about this party. New dress, new earrings . . . there's probably going to be royalty there."

"Sure is. *You.* Indulge me, Liz. I'm so proud of you, and it'll make me that much prouder to know that I've contributed something to all this."

She blushed. "I think you've lost your marbles."

He simply wiggled his brows, then pocketed the box with the earrings, took her arm and escorted her to a small sandwich shop near her office before he dropped her off.

That night she discovered precisely what personal somethings he'd bought during those ten minutes he'd been alone in the store. He waited until after they'd had dinner, until she stood in front of the bathroom mirror admiring the pearl earrings that, to her surprise and infinite relief, he'd had no trouble inserting. Then he disappeared and returned carrying the box, which he handed to her.

"This is for you."

"For me? But I thought—"

"I figured as much," he said with a grin. "Go ahead, open it."

She slid the top off and pressed back the layers of tissue, then bit her lip and shyly looked up.

"Not for the party," he instructed, but ever so gently, "or for me. Just for you."

The color rose in Liz's cheeks as she timidly touched the lace-and-silk confection of an ivory-hued bra, panties and matching slip.

"I want you to wear them," he went on in that same gentle tone, "just so you can see how super they look on you, so you can feel really...feminine, on the inside, privately. No one has to know they're there but you."

"I've never worn anything like this," she breathed. She didn't look at him because she felt slightly embarrassed, but she also felt excited and, yes, feminine.

"Then it's long overdue. You'd be amazed at what little nothings like these can do for the ego."

"You've had personal experience?" she teased, pleased to see his own cheeks grow red.

"Well, not in exactly the same way, but I do know that what I wear can make a difference in the way I feel. Right about now I'm feeling pretty stuffy because I've had to wear a suit all week. I'm really looking forward to going north. You've got plenty of jeans, don't you? And heavy sweaters—"

She cut him off with a laugh. "Yes, Donovan. I've got plenty for the country. And if I don't, I'm sure you'll shanghai me to the nearest sportswear store to rectify the situation."

"Would that be horrible?" he asked softly. "I really do love buying you things."

"I know," she said as softly, looking at him then, feeling her insides positively melt at the tenderness of his expression. "That's what makes receiving them so nice." She gave the lingerie a lingering caress. "Thank you for these . . . and for the dress . . . and the earrings. I do love them all."

He put his arms around her then and ran an adoring gaze over her face. "I'm glad. So glad," he murmured, kissing her gently before leading her back to the den, where they'd both left work they'd brought home from the office.

DONOVAN WAS THE ONE in for a surprise when he showed up at her office late Thursday afternoon to take her home. He walked in, then brought himself up short and stared. She'd been concentrating on a report when he arrived and had jerked her head up, then sat still, holding her breath.

He continued to stare, but his eyes widened, mirroring the growing smile on his face. "Your hair looks fantastic!" he breathed at last. "When did you do it?"

She shyly touched the ends, which barely reached her shoulders. "At lunchtime. Are you sure it looks okay? I feel naked. I think it's been hanging down to the middle of my back since I was eight."

"It looks unbelievable! And that's natural wave, isn't it?"

She blushed and nodded. "I didn't know I had it until the guy started cutting and there it was." She scrunched up her nose. "I'm not sure I like the front. I told him I didn't want bangs, but he insisted that I'd really outgrown a center part with everything hanging to one length. They're not really bangs, just kind of—" she gestured with her hand "—wispy things."

Beaming, Donovan walked toward her. "Whatever they are, they look great!" Unable to resist, he gently touched the shining brown tresses, first by her temples, then her crown, then her nape. "You look so soft." He cleared his throat of its frogginess. "I hope you know that this is going to do nothing for my peace of mind."

"It really looks okay?"

"More than okay. It looks beautiful, Elizabeth. I love it. I love *you*," he murmured as he dropped his head to give her a soft kiss. By the time he was done, he had to clear his throat again. "Uh, we'd better be going. Are you almost finished?"

It took Liz a minute to refocus, because his kiss had reawakened those little yearnings in her. She forced her eyes to the desk top, only to close the report she'd been reading. "I can finish in the morning."

So they headed home to change for the party.

Liz had had a hot bath and was finishing applying a touch of blusher and mascara—both new purchases—when Donovan called from the bedroom.

"Are you decent?"

She looked down and automatically crossed an arm over her breasts, then glanced back in the mirrow. Slowly and determinedly she lowered her arm.

"Yes."

The door swung open and Donovan sauntered in wearing his dark dress pants and a fine white shirt, which hung open. At the sight of her, he stopped short. His eyes ran over her breasts, which were delicately encased in the new bra, and her panties, outlined clearly beneath the slip. With a low moan he turned to the wall and put his forehead on the arm he braced there.

"Oh God," Liz breathed, distraught. "You don't like it."

"Just the opposite," was his deep groan. Very slowly he straightened, then as slowly turned to her. "The problem is that we might well not make it to that party at all. I thought you were dressed."

Self-consciously she looked down and frowned. "I guess I wanted you to see me . . . wearing these. . . ."

"I do," he rasped, taking her in trembling arms and pressing her full length against him. "I've been imagining it all day. Needless to say, I haven't gotten a helluva lot of work done."

Liz relaxed, then grew almost giddy. She did feel feminine at that moment. And sexy. And . . . almost beautiful.

"I'm glad," she whispered against the warmth of his throat. She felt the tension in him, but it was a good tension, and with her body molded to his as it was, the tension became an internal thing for her, as well.

He held her back and gave her a hungry look, then kissed her deeply and thoroughly. She was beginning to think that it wouldn't be so awful if they did miss the party when he wrenched his mouth away and dug into his trousers pocket.

"Here," he said hoarsely. "These go with the ear-rings."

Before she could know what he was up to, he had a single strand of pearls around her throat. He turned her to the mirror and stood behind her to fumble with the catch. His fingers were none too steady, and he swore once before he finally smoothed the beads down on her chest. Hands on her shoulders, he looked at her reflection.

Liz was entranced by the pearls. "They're beautiful," she whispered. "Too much. . . ."

"Not enough," he whispered back, lowering his mouth to her neck, where he pressed a series of soft kisses that had her closing her eyes and leaning back against him. "God, Liz, I want you so badly."

She could feel how badly, because his hips were arched against hers, but she could only concentrate on the gentle caress of his lips, then on his hands, which slid to cover her breasts. He lifted them, then kneaded softly, as she sighed at the flush of heat that spread through her.

He turned her in his arms and looked down at her, tracing her features with fingers that were light and shaking, sliding his hands down to her throat, then over the pearls to her breasts again. She felt an instinctive glimmer of apprehension, because he was watching his hands and what they touched, but that apprehension was soon overcome by the rising pleasure she felt. When he slipped his fingers inside the cups of her bra and explored the soft swelling of flesh there, a sound of delight escaped her lips.

"You're so lovely," he whispered, inching his fingers farther until they glanced past her nipples. "So lovely."

Eyes closed, she sighed his name. She wanted to touch him, too, but her hands were anchored on his shoulders if for no other purpose than to keep her upright. She nearly cried out in frustration when his fingers withdrew, but he was spreading his shirt open and lifting her against him.

"We have to leave," he rasped as though to remind himself, but he didn't release her. His hands were roaming her back, finally homing in on the catch of her bra, which he undid so quickly she could only gasp.

"It's okay, love. I just need to feel you against me. Just for a minute." The same hand was forward in an instant, tugging the bra up to her armpits. Her bare breasts touched his chest then, and the electricity of it curled through her. "See? It's wonderful . . . oh, Liz, I need you. Oh, God . . ."

She felt the same. Her body was coiled and trembling, and she suddenly wanted him to touch her all over, to kiss her all over, to finally relieve the awful knot of need so low in her belly.

But he was setting her back, replacing her bra and fastening it while she struggled to regain her composure. She was disappointed and frustrated.

"I...I thought you wanted me," she heard herself say. Such a short while ago she would have been appalled to hear the words, but she could only think of what he'd kindled, of what still burned.

Raking an unsteady hand through his hair, he gave her a crooked smile. "I do want you, but I want you to want me as badly."

"I do want you," she whispered.

"Not as badly. Not yet. When that time comes, you'll know. We'll both know." He took her face in his hands and kissed away her perplexed expression. "I love you, Liz. Keep that in mind while they're falling all over you tonight at the party."

THEY DIDN'T EXACTLY "fall over" her at the party, Liz mused, but the attention she got, the admiring glances didn't fail to stun her.

"It must be the dress...or the pearls," she murmured, when Donovan swept her away for a minute alone.

"It's not the dress or the pearls. It's *you*."

"I think it's *you*. I'm floating on the coattails of your charisma. I've never received compliments like these."

"You probably have, but you've ignored them. I know." He arched a pointed brow. "You ignored most of mine from the start. And don't give me that baloney about my charisma. You heard Donaldson. He said that old man Obermeyer never stops raving about you. I wouldn't be surprised if you get a new client out of this."

She blushed. "That wasn't why I came."

"I know that, but it'd be a nice side effect." He hooked a firm arm around her waist. "Come on. There's someone else I want you to meet. . . ."

When they got home that night, Donovan turned her to him. "Thank you for coming, Liz. You made me very happy. Were you? I mean, was it as bad as you thought it would be?"

She gave a soft laugh and looked down. "I wasn't expecting the worst."

"But you've said how you often feel at parties like that. Did you feel . . . awkward or outclassed?"

"No. Well, maybe just a little, once in a while."

"And the next time will be even better. It's all a matter of self-confidence, and that's bound to grow. I'm telling you, Liz, you had more going for you than any other woman in that room."

There was a tiny catch in her voice. "I don't know about that. There were some lovely women there—"

"Every one of whom you can compete with on the outside and none of whom can come close to you on the inside. As far as I was concerned, you were the only woman worth talking to in the room."

Liz studied his earnest expression. Indeed, he hadn't given more than a passing glance at another woman, and she'd been purposely looking to see if he would. "You made me feel special, Donovan. Thank you."

"You made my night. Thank *you*." He paused. An inkling of unsureness wrinkled his brow. "Let's go to bed," he said quietly, then added quickly, "Not to make love, just to be together. I want to be with you when you fall asleep tonight. Is that okay?"

She gave him a soft smile, then nodded. Even now the memory of what she'd felt earlier that evening was fresh in her mind, and with Donovan's tall, sturdy body so close to her she felt new waves of desire stirring. "I'd like that." She hesitated for an instant. "You can even . . . if you like . . ."

He draped an arm around her shoulders and led her down the hall. "What? And let you think I'm an easy lay? No way! I'd never make love to a woman after living with her for only four days. Nope. Tonight we'll sleep. Besides," he murmured more naughtily, "it'll take most of the night to do what I'd like, and we've both got to work tomorrow . . ."

Left unsaid was that tomorrow was Friday and they didn't have to work on Saturday.

THE DRIVE TO THE COUNTRY was slow, what with the weekend automotive exodus from the city and the snow that was lightly falling. By the time Donovan and Liz left the highway, the snow wasn't falling so lightly anymore and he was growing concerned.

"I'd like to go straight to the house, but if we don't make a stop at the supermarket, we may have to subsist on canned goods all weekend."

"We could make do. I'm sure you've got soup, and there must be things in the freezer."

"Yeah, but I really like fresh orange juice, and cereal's no good without milk."

He sounded like such a little boy at that minute that Liz couldn't help but laugh. So they did stop at the market, and by the time they reached the road leading to the house, Donovan was singing the praises of four-wheel drive. Four inches of snow had fallen, which wouldn't have been so terrible had the temperature not fallen even more quickly, turning the ground beneath the snow to a sheet of ice. He negotiated the twisting road with great care, and they both breathed a sigh of relief when at last they arrived at the house.

After they'd turned on the heat, built a fire and made dinner, they sat together in the loft watching a movie. Curled comfortably against Donovan, with an afghan spread liberally over them both, Liz tried to concentrate on the movie, but she couldn't. She felt happy and content, but restless, as well, for neither her mind nor her body could ignore the man who breathed so evenly nearby.

He'd been wonderful all week. He'd anticipated her needs, catered to them, respected them. He'd done everything in his power to let her know that he did truly find her attractive, that he did truly love her.

She wanted him. She wanted to touch him, to kiss him. She wanted him to do the same, and when she thought of that, she grew all the more restless. She marveled at the way he could lie there so unaffected, and she wondered if she was wrong, if he didn't really want her.

Tipping her head back so that she could study his face, she found her answer. A helpless smile spread across her features, and she felt a world of tenderness well up in her.

His dark lashes rested atop his cheekbones. His hair fell rakishly across his brow. His cheeks bore a slight flush. He was fast asleep.

"Donovan?" she whispered. "Donovan? Wake up." She gently shook his arm, rewarded when his eyes fluttered open. "You're exhausted. Why don't we go to bed?"

It took him a minute to realize where he was, and Liz grinned at the lost way he looked around.

"What happened?" he murmured groggily.

"You fell asleep is what happened." She threw back the afghan and pushed herself up, then reached for his hand. "Come on. To bed with you." She felt a little like a mother as she led him to the bedroom, but she kind of liked it. He'd taken such good care of her all week that she welcomed the chance to do something in return.

While Donovan stood by the side of the bed absently fumbling with his shirt buttons, she drew back the quilt and puffed the pillow, then turned to help him undress. Since she hadn't turned on a light for fear of disturbing his sleepy state, the room was in semidarkness, lighted only by the dusky glow of the snow outside. One part of her was grateful; she'd never undressed Donovan before and she felt vaguely self-conscious. The other part of her wanted to see more but had to settle for the faint outlines of his body. To her astonishment she discovered that these were as inflammatory to her senses as a fully lighted scene, for what the dimness failed to provide her imagination did. By the time he was stripped down to his shorts, she was trembling.

Dutifully she helped him into bed.

"You're coming, too, aren't you?" he mumbled, tugging the quilt to his armpits.

"In a minute," she whispered, then stood watching as his lids closed. He was beautiful lying there, his features in such thorough repose. Between his mussed hair and the shadow of his beard, he had the look of a rogue and the air of a child. It was a point in between that Liz craved.

Sighing, she turned and fished her nightgown from the drawer she'd set it in earlier. She closed the bathroom door behind her before she switched on the light and switched it off before she reemerged a few minutes later.

She padded softly to where Donovan lay and found that he hadn't moved. Gliding quietly around the bed, she pulled back the quilt on her side and settled gently down on the sheets. Rather than lie back, though, she turned her head to look again at the man beside her. He *was* beautiful, all the more so in the pale-blue light that should have been eerie but was somehow romantic.

Rising from the bed, she crept to the window. So cold outside . . . so warm inside. She thought of Donovan lying beneath the sheets in nothing but his shorts, and she grew even warmer, but in private places, places that had yet to know the fullest meaning of heat. She who hadn't dared once to dream now wanted so much . . . so much . . .

"Liz?"

His quiet voice came to her and her heart skipped a beat.

"Is something wrong, sweetheart?"

She turned and met his gaze. "No," she whispered. "I just . . ."

"Just what?"

She knew he couldn't possibly see the yearning in her eyes because it was so dark and there was still so much space separating them, and even if he did see it, she knew that he wouldn't push her to do what she didn't want to do. But she did—she did want him . . .

Quelling an unsteadiness born of anticipation, she slowly crossed the room to stand beside him. "Donovan, I . . . I . . ."

He was studying the way she twisted her hands together, the way her eyes were wide, almost pleading, the way her breath was coming in hesitant bursts. He knew what *he* wanted, and could only pray that she wanted the same. He raised the corner of the blanket in silent invitation that she join him, then held his breath.

He didn't have to hold it long—either his breath or the blanket—because she was quickly in bed with him and his arms were around her. "Oh, love," he gasped seconds before he captured her lips in a kiss she returned with the same hunger he felt. "Are you sure?" he whispered when at last he drew his head back.

She nodded.

"You do want me?"

She nodded again.

"As badly as I want you?"

She had only to feel the hardness of his body pressing against her and the answering thrill that surged through her to know that she did. "Yes."

A shudder went through him as he hugged her again. Then he rolled her to her back and moved over her, kissing her, pressing himself into her softness. He was gasping when he released her lips. "Slow. We'll . . . take it slow!" It was almost a command, and clearly directed at himself because he hadn't realized how fiercely his body would react to her simple yes.

He did kiss her more slowly, savoring every corner of her mouth, then the soft insides. Entwining his fingers with hers, he pressed her hands back to the sheets while he explored her face, her neck, her throat. Her hands remained where they were even when he released them to touch her breasts, and she was straining upward when he spoke again.

"Liz? Can I slip your nightgown off? You're so beautiful. I want to touch you."

A frisson of apprehension skipped through her, but she only had to look at his face and see the desire there to realize she wanted him, too. She nodded, then held her breath while he rolled off her and carefully eased the nightgown up over her thighs and her hips, then her waist and breasts, until it was over her head and discarded.

"There," he whispered as he reached up to unball her fists and hold her hands, "that wasn't so bad." Rather than take his time looking at her body, as she'd been afraid he might do, he eased over her again. Eyes closed, he tipped his head back. "Ahh. That feels so good. Oh, Liz, you can't imagine—"

But she could, because the feel of his nearly bare skin against hers was instantly rewarding. Her lips were parted when he caught them again, and he took a long while kissing her, letting her adjust to the feel of his warmth against hers. Only when he heard her soft, purring response did he slip to her side and very gently run a hand from her navel to her collarbone and back.

"I can't believe you're actually here," he murmured. His eyes followed the progress of his hand, but Liz didn't mind because he seemed so pleased and what he was doing felt so good. He continued to look at her and touch her, covering each of her breasts in turn before he bent his head and took one dark areola into his mouth.

Unprepared for the tugging sensation that ignited a fire to her womb, Liz gasped. But he continued to suck, raising his mouth only to touch the tip of his tongue to her nipple, and soon she was holding him closer, arching into his moist grasp, breathing raggedly.

His hands wandered farther then, coasting over her stomach to her thighs, returning over the juncture of her legs. With a quick indrawn breath, she pressed her knees together, but in an instant he was murmuring words of encouragement.

"It's okay, love. Let me touch you there. You're beautiful . . . every sweet inch." His hand crept lower again and began a slow, sensual stroking. "Relax, love. That's it. Open for me . . ."

She had no choice, because the fire there was so hot that she needed all the relief he could offer. Soon enough she learned that it was only temporary. Wherever his fingers delved the fire raged hotter, and she was clutching his waist, instinctively urging him toward her.

He paused only to rid himself of his briefs, and then he was back, tormenting her with his lips, his teeth, his tongue, his fingers.

"Donovan!" she breathed, unable to cope with the pleasure-pain a minute longer. Yet she did, for another minute, then two and more. Only when Donovan was satisfied that she was fully ready did he slide between her thighs.

"I love you, Elizabeth," he moaned as, with one magnificent thrust, he surged forward.

Liz cried out softly and arched her back in a reflexive attempt to escape the sharp pain of his entrance, but he held himself deeply embedded in her while he murmured soft, soothing words.

"That's it, love. It's done. The worst is over. Just relax. It'll ease."

She bit her lip against the shallow panting she couldn't control, but he was right. The pain was easing. He held himself still, filling her but demanding nothing. When he felt her thighs slowly fall back, he propped himself on his elbows and framed her face with his hands.

"I love you," he murmured between whispered kisses. "You have no idea how much." He drew his mouth over her eyes and brushed her lips with his thumbs. "Better?"

She gave a jerky nod. "I'm . . . sorry."

"For what?"

"For being such a ninny. It wasn't so bad...the pain."

"But it was sudden and it had to be, and *I'm* the one who's sorry about that," he crooned. "The wonderful thing is that it'll never be like that again. It only gets better and better. Do you believe me?"

She gave a short laugh. "I think I'd believe most anything you tell me since you've gotten me this far."

"And it is far, love. You're not a virgin anymore. You're mine now. All mine." He sealed the vow with a kiss that grew slowly seductive, then he began to touch her again, teasing her, coaxing her, stimulating her with his caresses until she was the one to move her hips in demand for his active possession.

Carefully he withdrew from her, then eased back inside, repeating the tempered motion until she joined it. From then on the pleasure spiraled for them both. From time to time he whispered endearments, but soon he was too caught up in her flame to do anything but gasp and drive onward.

As for Liz, she was whirling in an eddy of delight, reaching one plateau then surging to another higher and hotter. Stunned by the power of what she felt, she responded with an intuitive sense of rhythm. Her fingers dug into the slick muscles of his back, and she held on for dear life when she felt she would shatter into a million star-flung pieces.

"Donovan . . . ?" she cried, frightened at the end.

"Let it come, love. It's there. Let it come. I'll hold you."

He did, but it was for his own sake, as well, for with the first of her spasms his own body erupted, and he could think of nothing but clinging to this woman, to the pleasure she brought him, to the love he'd never known before and that he cherished nearly above life itself.

It was a long time before their harsh pants eased and either of them could speak. Donovan kissed the moistness from her brow and the tip of her nose, then slowly, reluctantly slid to the side and drew her to nestle against him.

"Oh, Donovan," she breathed, her smile audible even in that whisper. "I can't believe it."

He was smiling, too, then chuckling aloud. "It was good, wasn't it?"

"Good? No. It was fantastic!"

He chuckled again and hugged her tightly.

"Is it always that way?" she asked, rubbing her cheek against the damply curling hair on his chest.

"Not for everyone, especially the first time. For us, though, it'll always be as good, then better, and better, and better...I love you, Liz." When she tipped back her head and opened her mouth, he put a long finger against it. "Shh. Just let me say the words. If you say anything now, I'll always wonder if it was leftover passion or gratitude or simply sheer exhaustion. When you say those words to me, I want it to be at a time when I least expect it. But when you say them, you'd better mean them. Because as soon as I hear them, I'm going to ask you to marry me, and you'd better be prepared to say yes. Understood?"

Liz smiled against his finger, which had lingered to lightly stroke her lips. She knew that she loved him, but she also knew that he was right. When she said the words, she wanted them to carry the full weight they deserved. When she said them, she wanted to be able to say yes.

With a gentle kiss to his fingertip, she nodded, then settled down to enjoy the spanking new happiness of the moment.

10

THEY SPENT THE WEEKEND deliciously snowbound, if only in spirit since the plow came through Saturday morning and Donovan shoveled the walks that afternoon. Other than a frivolous romp in the snow on Sunday morning, though, they didn't budge.

The majority of their time was spent in a bed of one sort or another. They made love beneath the covers in the bedroom, on a pallet of cushions before the living-room fire, on the sofa in the loft. Donovan taught Liz the passionate art with the tenderness, the consideration that was so much a part of his nature. Ever aware of her ingrained self-consciousness, he conquered her body by steps until there was nothing she hid from his hands or his lips or his tongue. When she felt comfortable enough to stand nude with him in broad daylight, he was filled with pride and no small sense of victory.

He insisted she take long hot baths, then proceeded to join her and show her the pleasures of fluidity. More than once he took to massaging her aching muscles, only to have the massage end in another passionate bout. When Liz swore she would never walk again, he laughed and strolled out of the room, knowing she'd soon follow on his heels. Inevitably she did.

The woman who returned to Manhattan with him very early Monday morning was a far cry from the one who'd left there the Friday before. Liz glowed. She felt fulfilled in a very feminine way and more self-confident than she'd ever been before. True, that self-confidence always faltered a bit when she and Donovan were apart during the day, but their reunions were always so sweet that she gradually managed to control those daytime insecurities, as well.

Little by little she let slip to her friends that she was staying with Donovan. Where she'd half-suspected they'd be surprised that Donovan should remain interested in her, they weren't. Rather they accepted the news as though she fully deserved both him and the happiness he gave her. They were thrilled for her, and that fact bolstered her all the more.

As the weeks passed, Donovan took her out more and more, introducing her to his friends and business associates. On each instance he made her feel as though she was the best thing to ever come along in his life. His pride was boundless, as was his attentiveness. Never once did he so much as show a passing interest in another woman. It never ceased to amaze Liz that a perfectly beautiful woman could be standing next to him, yet he'd only have eyes for her.

Thus encouraged, she began to take more of the initiative when she was with him. More frequently she took on the cooking of dinner. She invited him to a get-together of several of her associates and their dates. She splurged on clothes and underthings, all of which were far more stylish than anything she'd bought before, and took new interest in her appearance.

In lovemaking, as well, she grew bolder, though in truth it came quite naturally. She was curious about

Donovan's body, wanting to explore him, to taste him, to discover what aroused him most. And since that arousal was very definitely two-way, she never once regretted her forwardness. Nor did Donovan. He called her a born seductress, and occasionally, when his body was limp and drained, bemoaned the Pandora's box he'd opened. But his words of love were always soon to follow, and Liz felt on top of the world.

Work-wise, their lives meshed as comfortably. Shortly before Christmas the Ullman merger went public, and though its attendant fanfare demanded much of their time, it was time spent together and therefore pleasurable. Donovan took the news of Ray Obermeyer's windfall in stride and even insisted on taking Liz and Cheryl to lunch one day to let the latter know he held no ill will toward her. Indeed, he laughed, he was almost grateful for what Ray had done, since it had brought Liz and him together. Liz blushed, but couldn't argue.

Where once Liz thought that her career had to take precedence over all else, now she found that she could easily arrange her schedule to accommodate the times she spent with Donovan. Karen Reynolds was a big help on that score, encouraging her to plan appointments for those days when she'd be in the city and to take paperwork with her when Donovan had to be in Troy.

Christmas came and went, and was the happiest one Liz could remember. She and Donovan spent it alone in the country house with a small, gaily decorated tree by the window and an ever-burning fire in the hearth. It was all the more meaningful, this time together, because two days later Donovan's son arrived and Liz temporarily moved back to her apartment.

It had been a mutual decision, given Donovan's growing relationship with his son, that David shouldn't be overwhelmed by the fact that his father was living with a woman. As it happened, though, Liz spent every free minute with the two of them, and at Donovan's insistance. It was almost as if he was more sure of himself when he was with her, and it worked out well all around. Donovan seemed more at ease with David, what with Liz's helping hand. David seemed more at ease with Donovan, what with not having every bit of his father's attention centered on him. Liz and David got along famously, such that by the time he boarded his plane to return home, David was instructing his father that he should marry Liz before losing her.

Donovan thought about that often. He hadn't mentioned marriage again, and Liz still hadn't said the words. But he no longer thought of their relationship in terms of a game with players making alternating moves. He and Liz were together, which had been his primary goal all along.

He knew that she loved him. He could see it in her eyes when she looked at him, feel it in her body when she made love to him. And there weren't any other men in her life—except her father and Jamie. The former was no problem. Though Liz hadn't been in touch with the elder Jerome, Donovan felt confident that Liz could hold her own now where her father and his perversities were concerned.

Jamie was another matter. Religiously Liz phoned him every week, and Donovan sensed that any qualms she might still have about herself related to the responsibility she felt for Jamie. She was always subdued for a few minutes after those calls, and though Donovan talked with her and tried to make her understand that she was doing everything she could for Jamie, certainly enough to cancel out the long-standing guilt she felt, he wasn't sure if he was getting through. It appeared that Liz was going to have to work things out for herself on that score, and all Donovan could do was love her, support her and wait.

THE WAIT WASN'T AS LONG as he'd feared it might be. Two weeks into January, on a Wednesday night shortly after he and Liz had arrived home, the phone rang. Donovan reached it first.

"Hello?"

There was a long silence, then a click. He replaced the receiver and headed for the kitchen after Liz, but within seconds the phone pealed again. He grabbed it from the wall just inside the kitchen door.

"Hello?"

Again there was a long silence.

"Hello!" he repeated, puzzled.

At last a man's voice came through, somewhat irritably giving the number he'd dialed and asking if he'd reached it.

"Yes," Donovan answered. "You've dialed correctly."

"But this is supposed to be Elizabeth Jerome's number."

Donovan felt a certain premonition. "It is. Hold on. I'll get her." He put the phone against his chest, then held it out to a questioning Liz.

"Hello?"

"Who was that?" a familiar voice asked.

She let out a sigh, then looked at Donovan. "Jamie. Hi! Is everything okay?" He never lifted his own phone to call her unless there was a problem, and she'd called him just the Sunday before.

"Who *was* that, Liz?"

"That? Uh, that was Donovan Grant."

"Who's he?"

"The man I've been seeing."

Jamie laughed, but it had a sneering twist. "That's a new one. I didn't think you dated."

"I do."

"What's he doing at your apartment?" The tone was definitely one of demand, almost indignation, rather than brotherly concern.

Liz felt her hackles rising, but she couldn't quite come out with the truth. Jamie needed time. "Where are you? You sound very close."

"I am very close. I'm at the airport."

"Here?" She paled, and Donovan put a gently supportive hand on her shoulder. "*Is* something wrong?"

"Nah. Work's just getting to me, so I thought I'd take a while off."

"Oh, no, Jamie. You haven't been let go, have you?"

"I may just quit, but I haven't been fired yet. This is vacation time, which my boss is generous enough to dole out." His sarcasm did nothing for Liz's peace of mind.

"Okay. Vacation is fine. After you've had a break you'll feel better about things."

He didn't address that particular issue, but was obviously more concerned for his immediate well-being. "I thought I'd stay with you for a couple of days. You're not running out of town, are you?"

"Uh, no."

"Good. I'll be over soon."

"Jamie, maybe—Jamie?" She waited, then slowly replaced the phone and looked up at Donovan. "He hung up. He's on his way to my apartment."

Donovan gently kneaded her shoulders, easing them back when they tried to slump forward. "That's okay, love. He can stay there."

"But he'll expect me to be there."

He spoke after a minute's pause. "You could."

"No! I want to be here with you, not there. But I'll have to tell Jamie where I am and why."

"You don't owe him elaborate explanations, Liz," he reminded her quietly, repeating arguments he'd used before. "You're an adult. So is he. You've got every right to live your own life."

She hung her head. "I know."

"Listen, put your coat on and I'll take you over. You can let Jamie in and get him settled. We can even take him to dinner. Then you and I can come back here. Jamie will be fine. He's used to being alone."

"I know, which is one of the reasons I feel so awful. I'm the only family he's got. I'll feel guilty leaving him alone when he's here."

"But you say you don't want to stay there."

"I don't!"

"So we can do second best. We can spend time with him in the evenings. I can get tickets to a show or, if you can bear it, a basketball game."

That drew a tentative if sheepish smile from her. "You were right about that, y'know. It's not such an awful game once you get to know it. And since I've had to sit through—" she eyed the ceiling "—how many televised games? Seven? Eight?"

"Is that a complaint?" he drawled, eyes twinkling.

Liz stood on tiptoe and cinched her arms around his neck. "No. It's not a complaint. I love hearing you cheer for your team!" She kissed his cheek and let herself down. "Okay. Let's go to my place. I might as well get this over with."

Within ten minutes they were at her apartment, turning on the lights and increasing the heat, then waiting until Jamie arrived twenty minutes later. His hair was as unruly as ever, but he was dressed neatly and this time carried a suitcase. Self-consciously Liz introduced Donovan, whom Jamie had been staring at since he'd entered. She knew she saw annoyance in his eyes, perhaps cynicism, but she reminded herself, as she had earlier, that he simply needed time to adjust to the change in her status.

At Donovan's suggestion they went out for dinner, and if Jamie was less than gracious, Donovan made up for it, doing everything he could to coax the sullen expression from the younger man's face. Liz was conscious of Jamie glaring at her from time to time, but she made no mention of the fact that she wouldn't be staying with him until they'd returned to her apartment. Then, it seemed, she had no choice.

"Well, uh, listen, Jamie," she began, knotting her fingers tightly together, "you can have the run of the place for as long as you want. I'll, uh, I'll be staying at Donovan's."

Jamie looked utterly dumbfounded. "You'll what?"

"I'll be staying with Donovan."

"Hey, listen, Lizzie. You don't want to do that. I've never needed the place to myself before. And it wouldn't be much fun for Donovan to be imposed upon that way."

"It's not an imposition," Donovan stated. He'd just about exhausted his supply of graciousness for the night, and he didn't like Jamie's tone of voice.

"What Donovan means," Liz hurried to explain, "is that I've been staying with him for a while now."

Jamie darted a cursory glance around the apartment. "What's the matter? This place low on heat or running water or something?"

"No. It's fine. I've chosen to live with Donovan."

"Why would you do a thing like that?" His gaze narrowed. It wasn't that he was being purposely obtuse, Liz knew, just that he had a very specific view of her. "Are you getting crank calls or something? Is it the protection you need? If that's the case, I'll be here—"

"That's *not* the case," Liz interrupted more firmly. She was aware of Donovan standing close, growing more tense by the minute, and the last thing she wanted was an unpleasant exchange between the two. "You don't understand. Donovan and I are *living* together."

Jamie stared at her, his eyes wide, then he threw back his head and laughed. "That's a good one, Liz. I never thought I'd hear that coming from you."

"Why ever not?" she asked. Strangely, she'd known how Jamie would react, yet now that he'd done so she felt a slow anger burning inside her.

"I mean, look, Liz, you're not exactly a temptress."

"Now, just a minute—" Donovan gritted, only to be restrained by Liz's tight grip on his arm.

"I'll handle this, Donovan. Jamie, go on. Say what you mean."

"Come on, Lizzie. You've never been a looker. You were the perennial wallflower back home, and you've lived the life of a nun since you left. Do you honestly expect me to believe that you've taken a lover—or, more to the point, that he's taken *you*?"

"That's exactly what I expect you to believe," Liz ground out. "I also expect—have a *right* to expect—that you'll be happy for me."

"Right? What right do you have? Damn it, you heard Dad, Liz. You're nothing—"

"That's enough!" Donovan exploded, but again Liz kept him from saying more. Her tone was taut, but quiet.

"Let me handle this, Donovan. There's an awful lot I have to say to Jamie, and it's long overdue." She turned to her brother, one arm stiff by her side, the other connecting to Donovan's arm as though, despite her disclaimer, she needed the lifeline.

"Dad was wrong, Jamie. Dead wrong. I've finally come to see that, thanks to Donovan."

Jamie gave an ugly laugh. "Donovan? What could he ever see in you?"

"I've asked myself the same question a hundred times, and there are times when I still ask it, when I can't quite believe the answer. But Donovan does, and that's what matters. He loves me, Jamie. He loves me despite every little fault I've got!" When Donovan started to argue, she squeezed his arm in a bid for silence. "And what would be so awful, from your point of view, if he loves me? It doesn't change the way I feel toward you. It doesn't change the fact that I'll continue to love you, to help you whenever I can. You don't have to be threatened by Donovan. I was for weeks, until I realized how foolish it was."

"I'm not *threatened* by him."

"Then why are you so upset that I'm living with him?"

"I'm not upset. I'm just...shocked. You...living with someone like him...it's incredible."

"What do you mean, 'someone like him'?" she spat. It was one thing for Jamie to insult her, quite another for him to attack Donovan. As it happened, in her rush to defend Donovan she'd misinterpreted Jamie, who proceeded to set her straight.

"Oh, there's nothing wrong with him," Jamie said impudently. "In fact, I got the impression from what he said over dinner that he's got a hell of a lot going for him. Which is what makes it all so astounding. He's good-looking and successful. He can have any woman he wants. That he should choose you..." He shook his head for effect.

Donovan couldn't keep still. "Liz, I think we ought to go. You don't need this—"

"No, Donovan. There's more I have to say." She turned back to Jamie and her soft voice took on a sheath of steel. "You know, you've been putting me down for years. Oh, maybe more subtly than Dad did, but it's always been there. You've held me responsible for everything you've suffered, and maybe I'm to blame because I let you do it. I've lived with guilt for so long—guilt at thinking that I might have somehow spared you Dad's beatings—"

"Damn it, Liz!" Jamie cut in, slicing an angry glance at Donovan. "Not in front of him!"

But Liz was livid. "He knows it all, but that's beside the point. The point *is* that there *wasn't* anything I could have done to help you. I took my own beatings, Jamie. Where were *you* when I could have used help?"

"I was just a kid!"

"*So was I!* I suffered then, and I suffered long after, and never once have you given me support or understanding or encouragement. No, you let me go on believing everything Dad said, seeing myself as the ugly little nothing he seemed to think I was. But I'm through now. I've had it. Evidently your Dr. Branowitz hasn't done all that much, if he's never gotten going on your feelings toward me. Or maybe he simply takes your word and honestly believes I'm the dog you think I am. Well, *I'm not!*"

Fury had her shaking all over, but she wasn't about to stop. "We're all grown up now, Jamie, and I for one need to put the past to rest. I may never be a looker, as you call it, but I'm not ugly and repulsive, and I'm not some kind of freak. I've got friends who like me and business associates who respect me, and Donovan who loves me. And you know something? *I love him!*" Her expression still cross, she looked at Donovan. "The answer is yes."

Then she turned back to Jamie, but her tone gradually softened. "I love him, and I'm going to marry him, and it would make me very happy to know that you can accept it, that you can come to like both of us. Because I do love you, Jamie. You're my only brother. I'd like you to share some of what Donovan and I have. Our life is going to be wonderful, far different from anything you and I ever knew, and we'd like it if you could be with us sometimes. If you find you can't, then I'll accept that and move on, because nothing, *nothing*, is going to cast a shadow on the rest of my life. I've lived in the dark for too long. And so have you. Think about it, Jamie."

When Donovan put an arm around her shoulder, she looked up at him and smiled. The pride in his face was as unmistakable as the love, and she felt suddenly lightheaded and free.

"He's got you brainwashed," Jamie muttered.

"Well," Liz mused serenely, hooking her arm through Donovan's and starting for the door, "If that's so, I love it. Because I've never been happier in my life."

"DID YOU MEAN IT?" Donovan asked, crowding her against the wall just outside her building.

"Every word. Boy, did that feel good!"

"You do love me?"

"I do love you."

"And you'll marry me?"

"In a minute."

"It'll have to be longer than that. There's a tiny matter of the law to contend with."

Liz's eyes widened. "The law?" She couldn't help but recall the fateful instrument of their union.

Donovan grinned and popped a kiss on her nose. "Not *that* law. The one governing things like blood tests and licenses and marriages in the eyes of the Lord and the state of New York."

She laughed and threw her head back. "*That* law. Well, I'll leave all that to you. You're the one who's got friends in high places. But I'm telling you, buddy, if you lean into me any closer you may have to worry about charges of indecency. I don't think they allow love-making on the streets of New York."

"Mmm. I think you're right. Come on. Let's go home."

"Now that's the best idea you've had all night."

ACTUALLY, IT WASN'T, but Liz didn't find out about the other until she got out of her bath and went looking for Donovan. He was walking down the hall toward the bedroom when she emerged.

"Where were you?" she asked softly. "I was beginning to worry."

"I just called Jamie."

"You did?"

"I'm meeting him for lunch at the office tomorrow."

"You don't have to do that, Donovan."

"But I do. You're still angry at him, but by tomorrow you'll be feeling badly. *I* feel badly. All things considered, Jamie must be feeling lost. He's had some mean shakes in life, and he's bound to be thrown by what he sees as your defection. I'm not sure how much of what you said tonight he absorbed, especially the part about his being welcome to spend time with us, but I want to reinforce it. I don't know if it'll do any good, but I don't think I'd forgive myself if I didn't give it a try."

For a minute Liz was speechless. Then she threw her arms around Donovan's neck and hugged him tightly. "Have I ever told you how wonderful you are?"

"That's not what I need to hear. It's those other words . . ."

"I love you? I love you . . . love you . . . love you . . ."

She was still chanting when he lifted her in his arms and carried her to bed.

HARLEQUIN SUPERROMANCE®

A PLACE IN HER HEART...

Somewhere deep in the heart of every grown woman is the little girl
she used to be....

In September, October and November 1992, the world of childhood
and the world of love collide in six very special romance titles. Follow
these six special heroines as they discover the sometimes heart-
wrenching, always heartwarming joy of being a Big Sister.

Written by six of your favorite Superromance authors, these
compelling and emotionally satisfying romantic stories will earn a
place in your heart!

SEPTEMBER 1992

#514 NOTHING BUT TROUBLE—Sandra James
#515 ONE TO ONE—Marisa Carroll

OCTOBER 1992

#518 OUT ON A LIMB—Sally Bradford
#519 STAR SONG—Sandra Canfield

NOVEMBER 1992

#522 JUST BETWEEN US—Debbi Bedford
#523 MAKE-BELIEVE—Emma Merritt

AVAILABLE WHEREVER
HARLEQUIN SUPERROMANCE
BOOKS ARE SOLD

HARLEQUIN®

Temptation

Rebels & Rogues

Trey: He lived life on the edge . . . and wasn't about to be tamed by a beautiful woman.

THE RED-BLOODED YANKEE!
By Ruth Jean Dale
Temptation #413, October

All men are not created equal. Some are rough around the edges. Tough-minded but tenderhearted. Incredibly sexy. The tempting fulfillment of every woman't fantasy.

When it's time to fight for what they believe in, to win that special woman, our Rebels and Rogues are heroes at heart. Twelve Rebels and Rogues, each month in 1992, only from Harlequin Temptation. Don't miss the upcoming books by our fabulous authors such as Janice Kaiser and Kelly Street.

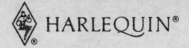 HARLEQUIN®

THE TAGGARTS OF TEXAS!

Harlequin's Ruth Jean Dale brings you
THE TAGGARTS OF TEXAS!

Those Taggart men—strong, sexy and hard to resist...

You've met Jesse James Taggart in FIREWORKS!
Harlequin Romance #3205 (July 1992)

Now meet Trey Smith—he's THE RED-BLOODED YANKEE!
Harlequin Temptation #413 (October 1992)

Then there's Daniel Boone Taggart in SHOWDOWN!
Harlequin Romance #3242 (January 1993)

And finally the Taggarts who started it all—in LEGEND!
Harlequin Historical #168 (April 1993)

Read all the Taggart romances!
Meet all the Taggart men!

Available wherever Harlequin books are sold.

TAKE A LESSON FROM RUTH LANGAN, BRONWYN WILLIAMS, LYNDA TRENT AND MARIANNE WILLMAN...

A *history* lesson! These and many more of your favorite authors are waiting to sweep you into the world of conquistadors and countesses, pioneers and pirates. In Harlequin Historicals, you'll rediscover the romance of the past, from the Great Crusades to the days of the Gibson girls, with four exciting, sensuous stories each month.

So pick up a Harlequin Historical and travel back in time with some of the best writers in romance.... Don't let history pass you by!

WELCOME TO
TYLER

The quintessential small town, where everyone
knows everybody else!

Finally, books that capture the pleasure
of tuning in to your favorite TV show!

Join your friends at Tyler in the eighth book, BACHELOR'S PUZZLE by Ginger
Chambers, available in October.

*What do Tyler's librarian and a cosmopolitan architect have in common? What
does the coroner's office have to reveal?*

GREAT READING...GREAT SAVINGS...
AND A FABULOUS FREE GIFT!

Each book set in Tyler is a self-contained love story; together, the twelve novels
stitch the fabric of the community. You can't miss the Tyler books on the shelves
because the covers honor the old American tradition of quilting; each cover
depicts a patch of the large Tyler quilt!

And you can receive a FABULOUS GIFT, ABSOLUTELY FREE, by collecting
proofs-of-purchase found in each Tyler book, *and* use our Tyler coupons to save
on your next TYLER book purchase.

If you missed *Whirlwind* (March), *Bright Hopes* (April), *Wisconsin Wedding* (May), *Monkey
Wrench* (June), *Blazing Star* (July), *Sunshine* (August) or *Arrowpoint* (September) and would
like to order them, send your name, address, zip or postal code, along with a check or money
order for $3.99 (please do not send cash), plus 75¢ postage and handling ($1.00 in Canada)
for each book ordered, payable to Harlequin Reader Service, to:

In the U.S.

3010 Walden Avenue
P.O. Box 1325
Buffalo, NY 14269-1325

In Canada

P.O. Box 609
Fort Erie, Ontario
L2A 5X3

Please specify book title(s) with your order.
Canadian residents add applicable federal and provincial taxes.

TYLER-8